ISTVÁN ÖRKÉNY

# more
# one minute st

ISTVÁN ÖRKÉNY

# more
# one minute stories

selected & translated by
judith sollosy

PREFACE
PÉTER ESTERHÁZY

CORVINA

This collection of *More One Minute Stories*
has been compiled from the following volumes:
István Örkény, *Egyperces novellák*, Magvető Kiadó Budapest 1977
*Egyperces novellák*, Szépirodalmi Könyvkiadó Budapest 1985
*Búcsú, Kiadatlan novellák*, Szépirodalmi Könyvkiadó Budapest 1989
and *Egyperces novellák*, Palatinus Budapest 2001.



*Fourth edition, 2015*

This edition published by Corvina Books, Ltd.,
Dankó u. 4-8, 1086 Budapest, Hungary
e-mail: corvina@lira.hu

ISBN 978 963 13 6307 4

# contents

9 preface: some short paragraphs about a great writer by Péter Esterházy
15 the grotesque
17 humoresque
19 "torschlusspanik"
21 free will
23 károly keleti
25 memoirs of a puddle
26 fellow citizens
27 birthday greetings
29 a bright and distant future
32 notices and announcements
34 asylum
38 information
39 tulip in crisis
41 who is the sinner?
42 our wildest dreams can come true
44 gravepost
45 the meaning of life
46 thoughts from the cellar
47 spectacular christmas sale
51 who writes the one minute stories? you or I?
56 slaughterhouse
58 immortality
59 we're an equestrian nation
61 gli ungheresi
63 encounter
66 bad dream
69 one wednesday morning
73 news and pseudo-news
78 the laundress's dream

82 hidden talent
83 honeymooners on flypaper
86 hungarian moon rocket back on earth
90 historical mistake
91 the quick and effective clearing up of an embarrassing historical mistake
92 headlines
93 meat loaf
94 the age of aggression
95 aiming for the salt cellar
100 four theses
102 homo sapiens
104 ballad about the magic of poetry
107 when it comes to the most complicated matters…
110 embarrass de richesses
112 hungaricum
113 has anyone seen…?
114 empty page
115 inventory
116 so much to keep in mind
117 except for you
118 I buy my book
122 the death of the viewer
124 what is art?
128 no sooner is one dilemma solved than another rears its ugly head
129 for a keepsake album
130 a grain of rice laments
135 the final question
139 prose poems
139 ballad about the first world war
140 ballad about homesickness
141 ballad about the bombing of Budapest
141 ballad about emigration
142 ballad about sleepless nights
142 ballad about the truth
144 ballad about the working class
146 new saying
148 folklore
149 new lords
150 what gives?

153 triplets in óbuda
157 a quick lesson in foreign affairs
160 my good old fellow
163 snowy landscape, two onion domes
165 paris, à bientôt!
167 banner
168 perpetuum mobile
170 let's learn foreign languages
174 appetite
176 in memoriam dr. h.g.k.
177 home sweet home
178 the best of all possible worlds
179 survival
181 fate
182 the long march
184 our sons
185 tempting providence
187 the hallowed halls of science
189 the old man and the great big automobile
191 room, adobe wall, thatched roof
193 the loudspeaker
195 final solution
197 the relativity of fear
199 the people of técső
202 budapest
204 one minute biography

# some short paragraphs about a great writer

Unless my memory plays me false, when István Örkény's one minute stories were first published, there was no Central-Europe yet, just Eastern-Europe; in short, there was what was, except we didn't talk about it yet. (*Definition:* Central-Europe – Eastern-Europe at the peak of its popularity.) As soon as they appeared, the stories became wildly popular and were passed on in company as if they'd been jokes; they were sung as if they'd been folk songs; and the youthful barbers' assistants whistled them on the street as if they'd been from *La Traviata*. And if anyone recited the latest from memory, his chances of getting the girl (boy, etc.) grew by leaps and bounds.

And if we wondered, along with our best friend, what our latest girlfriend, "gorgeous, a looker, if ever there was one," was otherwise missing, there was nothing for it, we had to give the verdict by resorting to the quintessential Örkény sentence, "A heart," that's what she's missing. "She has a slender figure, fine curves and a flawless complexion. But something, and don't be offended, for God's sake, yes, something, minor, of no consequence, really, is missing from her all the same." "Yes, a heart."

The Eastern-European negotiated his way around the grotesque with ease. No, I take that back, not with ease, just naturally. It was second nature to him. The Eastern-European absurd is the genre par excellence of the sixties and early seventies, and it fed on the vertiginous contrast between seeming and reality; this is what Mrozek, Hrabal, Örkény, Konrád (with his *The Visitor*), Páral, Fuks, Havel, Sorescu, Róyewicz cried, sobbed, laughed and guffawed as they compiled an inventory of the contradictions around them with a pleasure mixed with pain, pain mixed with a sense of playfulness. Though we could have done without the "given reality" that was our form of life, it was incredibly interesting. (I might add as an aside that the story continued with us getting bored with this give and take of seeming and reality, this resplendent and hideous hide-and-seek, where we were the experimental white mice. We got bored with it, and that was its grotesque end. What remained was irony – naturally, of the constructive type, of which Musil speaks.)

The heart that is missing is from the story "Merry-Go-Round", written in the 1930s.* The grotesque was the young Örkény's natural voice (he was born in 1912), but he abandoned it and did not return to it until thirty years on. At the risk of sounding ludicrous, we might say that neither the war nor Communist dictatorship could bring anything new to bear on Örkény's works, and yet it so happens that it was the war and the two dictatorships that provided the seed, the silence, the horror that proved to be the source on which Örkény's art fed.

The short letter he wrote from the Russian front to a friend is a one minute story in itself: "I don't get to the opera as often as I'd like. I'm too busy crawling on my belly, wiping out my fellow men."

Örkény did not get home from the Russian prisoner of war camp until late in 1946 ("I saw death, where human morals

* The piece is included in *One Minute Stories,* Brandl & Schlesinger, Sydney and Corvina, Budapest, first printed in 1994.

stop, from up close many times") only to be swept along by the vicissitudes of Eastern-European history. Here, too, I'll just mention an anecdote. At the time, Örkény was working as a sort of socialist-realist newspaper reporter writing about the "building of socialism". He's just making a report about a foundry to be opened soon, when the elderly man providing him with information learns that he's the son of the famous Österreicher pharmacist, whereupon he calls him aside and, pointing to the gigantic construction work, he confidentially says, "It's horse's balls we're going to cast here, Comrade Österreicher, not steel!" The sentence was not included in the report, but it has survived all else from those years. It is a relevant and practical sentence. It is bristling with life.

The one minute stories are also vitally alive. They are not "old" texts, not just possibly interesting broadcasts about a bygone time and regime. In an interview, Péter Nádas said that for him, reading Örkény is like "bathing in the ocean, provided we think of the ocean as something infinite and beyond reach, seeing how Hungary does not have an ocean."

The one minute stories are both the ocean and the Hungarian shallows, cosmic, while providing an authentic introduction to Hungarian history and the Hungarian mentality. And this (naturally) brings us to the genre. A one minute story by Örkény is an enigmatic entity. It is not just short prose but is a combination of many things, anecdote (and I do not mean the Hungarian variety that always likes to think of itself as the victor, and is therefore the genre of light-hearted self-delusion, but, rather the Czech variety, which contains more self-irony and laughter at ourselves); aphorism, short note, found object, tale, joke, parable, a little of everything; Kafka, except Örkény's parables are also parodies; there is more lyricism in Daniil Charman, while Peter Bichsel is more domestic. Örkény is in flight, and his dignity comes from the fact that he knows there is nowhere to flee. We, Hungarian writers, are bound to him by countless ties. As far as his use of the language is concerned, Örkény belongs to the Kosztolányi-type of purist prose. It utterly lacks in sentimentality, which brings to mind the greatest of sober writers, Miklós Mészöly, let's say, and so does the austerity of his texts, the unadorned severity of his sentences. He is engaged in the hopeless (Hungarian) struggle for clarifying concepts, and in this Nádas is Örkény's pupil, while the use of our deteriorating everyday speech has encouraged the writer of these lines – encouraged to be himself. I hear Örkény even from behind the relentless irony of Kertész.*

Legend has it that a colleague of mine once asked Ferenc Puskás** how it was possible that his ball always landed where he wanted. "It's gotta be aimed like that, old man," Puskás was supposed to have said – a great Hungarian philosopher. This is why Örkény could be an inspiration to other writers. You could tell that he aimed it "like that".

Örkény does not tell it, he comes out and says it. What he writes is philosophy, i.e., thinking, but not abstract. It is witty, but not convivial. Keen, unsparing, brutal – poetic. Wry,

* Dezső Kosztolányi (1885-1936), the author of *Anna Édes, Nero the Bloody Poet*, and other novels. He was also a renowned translator; Miklós Mészöly (1921-2001) in his lifetime was considered the preeminent modern Hungarian prose stylist; Péter Nádas (b. 1942) is a major Central European literary figure who made his international breakthrough with his monumental novel, *Book of Memories* (written in 1986). Imre Kertész (b. 1929), won the Nobel Prize for Literature for his novel, *Fateless*, in 2002.

** Ferenc Puskás (b. 1927), also known as the "Galloping Major", was the star of the Hungarian national soccer team for years. He was known to possess a ferocious left-footed shot that led his team to victory after victory.

like the English, elegant, like the French, consistent, like the Germans – Hungarian. After Márai, the only bourgeois. (And Nádas after him.) Cartesian order and faith, *quia absurdum,* disillusionment and good cheer. The pathos of disillusionment. "Long live the question mark, down with the period."

From time to time, the one minute stories resemble post-Auschwitz poems that can't be written. In his review of a Semprun book,* Martin Lüdke writes that Semprun almost got into trouble in camp because of his intimate knowledge of German culture. Of course, thanks to Örkény's one minute story entitled "In memoriam Dr. H.G.K." the Hungarian reader has known this for years.

*"Hölderlin ist ihnen unbekannt?"* Dr. H.G.K. asked as he dug the pit for the horse's carcass.

"Who is that?" the German guard growled.

"The author of *Hyperion,*" said Dr. H.G.K., who had a positive passion for explanations. "The greatest figure of German Romanticism. How about Heine?" he tried again.

"Who're them guys?" the guard growled again.

"Poets," Dr. H.G.K. said. "But Schiller. Surely you have heard of Schiller?"

"That goes without saying," the German guard said.

"And Rilke?" Dr. H.G.K. insisted.

"Him, too," the German guard said and, turning the color of paprika, shot Dr. H.G.K. in the head.

By now, the – how shall I put it – ontological absurdity of the world has been replaced by the absurdity of our Mondays and Tuesdays. The one minute stories, too, glide between

* Jorge Semprun (b. 1923), like Kertész, was in a concentration camp and has devoted his life to writing about the Holocaust and post-Holocaust experience.

heaven and earth in the same way. The incredible becomes credible, which is – clearly – incredible. "What gives?" This is Örkény's fundamental question. But even if we don't have the answer, we are that we are – unique.

"Who are you, you lovely, long haired, slender young maiden?"

"My full name is Klára Nóra Annamária Olga Vorazlicki. But they call me Noodle. And who are you, old man?"

"My name is also Klára Nóra Annamária Olga Vorazlicki, and they also call me Noodle."

"How curious. You're old, bald, and your right eye is stuck all the way up in its socket. I don't think I understand."

"You must learn, Noodle, that there are no two identical Klára Nóra Annamária Olga Vorazlickis in the world."

"What a shame!"

"And so it is."

What gives? Yes, what gives?

A sad, much suffering man, this is how I have always thought of him. That he is my contemporary. That he is an Eastern-European so *ab ovo,* he knows a great deal. A great deal and – *ab ovo* – not enough. I thought I could see all this on his heavy, furrowed, smiling face. He died over twenty-five years ago, in 1979. This is when we are most apt to forget a writer. Örkény is the great exception.

Needless to say, I wouldn't want to talk the reader into anything; it's just that I see no reason *not* to read this book. He had as many wrinkles on his face as my grandmother. If we were inside a novel now, I'd say, exactly the same number of wrinkles. I know. I counted them.

*Péter Esterházy*

# the grotesque

*(a practical approach)*

Stand with your legs apart. Bend forward all the way. Look back between your legs. Thank you.

Now look around you and take stock of what you see. The world has been stood on its head. The gentlemen's feet beat about in the air while the ladies, see how they grab for their skirts? The cars, too: their four tires are spinning in the air, looking for all the world like a dog trying to scratch its stomach. Then there's the chrysanthemum, its thin jack-in-the-box stem reaching for the sky as it balances precariously on its head – and the express train speeding along on top of its trail of smoke.

To the left, the parish church stands balanced on the tips of the lightning rods sticking out of its twin steeples. And over there is a sign on the window of a pub:

**FRESH BEER ON TAP**

Inside, a customer, his head to the floor, staggers laboriously from the counter, holding a mug of beer in his hand. Do notice the order, though: the foam is at the bottom, the beer is on the top, and the bottom of the mug is on top of the beer. Yet not a drop is spilled.

Is it winter? You bet your life! Just look at the snowflakes, how they are fluttering up, and the skaters as they zigzag in pairs, dangling from the icy mirror of the sky. Not an easy sport, skating!

However, let us look for a merrier spectacle. Ah, there! A funeral! Amidst the snowflakes falling up, through the veil of tears trickling the other way around, we can see the gravediggers haul the coffin up with two hefty ropes. The colleagues, friends and relations of the deceased, both near and far, his widow and three orphans all grab some clods of earth and begin pelting the coffin. Let us recall the heartrending sound as the clods of earth are flung into a grave, knock against the coffin and break into tiny little pieces. The grieving widow sobs. The poor fatherless orphans wail.

How different it feels to throw things up! How much more dexterity it takes to hit the coffin! To start with, you need high quality clods, otherwise they disintegrate halfway up. So there is much grabbing, shoving and running helter-skelter to retrieve the most compact pieces. But a good clod of earth is not enough. Badly aimed, it falls back down and if it should hit somebody, especially a rich, distinguished relative, there is no escaping the titter of delight that follows. However, if all goes well and the clod of earth is firm and compact, the aim is accurate and on the mark, the man who flung it is applauded, and everyone goes home feeling happy. For days to come people talk about the perfect aim, the charming deceased, and the amusing ceremony, how splendid it turned out, and they do so with no trace of hypocrisy, feigned lamentation or pretense at sympathy.

And now, you may straighten up. As you see, the world is on its feet again, and you are at liberty to mourn your dearly departed with all the tears and dignity you can muster.

# humoresque

My daughter must have been around four or five when she tripped, fell, and hit her head. Before she could start crying, I suddenly thought of something funny to make her smile. But she didn't. She just pulled a long face and announced, "It's funny only if Angela laughs!" This definition defies the ravages of time.

Let's translate this into the language of literature. If readers laugh we've got a comedy, if they fall off their seats laughing we've got a farce, and if they smile, we've got sagacious, understated humor.

Mind you, these differences are not about quality but about quantity, and provided that my daughter Angela was right, humor includes all sorts of responses, from a smile to a belly laugh. To the best of my knowledge, no one else has ever demanded such unilateral, one-sided response from writing of any other kind, i.e., from writing that is not humorous. Anyone watching *Hamlet*, for instance, is free to decide for himself whether he'd rather fall to reflection or plummet into despair, give in to short, though pleasant spells of slumber or, having been purified, hurry home to start a new life. Someone watching *Hamlet* feels whatever he chooses to feel, depending on his character, disposition, or momentary state of mind.

At a concert performance of Beethoven's *Ninth Symphony,* the full scale of the human soul is sounded. Under the circumstances, a concert-goer would stand out only if he laughed.

In sharp contrast, humor allows for just one kind of response. In its unilateral effect humor is like a laxative except – biologically speaking – it brings a much more complex process into play. Whether we like it or not, a burlesque will make us laugh until we're fit to burst. When faced with a burlesque, a man would have to stare blank-eyed into space and heave a woeful sigh to make a spectacle of himself.

Since people are of many kinds and laugh for many reasons, anyone who decides to write humorous prose pieces will have a much harder time of it than his fellows, who opt for writing non-humorous prose.

This is just beginning to dawn on me now, as I write this humoresque, and I feel a dull pain around my heart when I think that a reader might read these lines with a bitter countenance, and tears rolling down his cheeks.

Is this fair? No.

Can anything be done about it? No.

Is there a remedy? No.

Should I stop writing? Yes.

But despite this forceful line of reasoning, I have no intention of laying down my pen. I am hoping that, willy-nilly, I will achieve the desired effect, which in its one-sidedness is so difficult to achieve, but which I hope to achieve all the same. And if I fail, I can still console myself with the thought that I, at least, smiled as I wrote these lines and will continue to smile as I correct them, and I will smile in the future, too, when I recall them. In which case, of course, I should revise my daughter's definition as follows:

It's funny only if the writer laughs.

# "torschlusspanik"

Franz Liszt, the fifty-seven-year-old snowman (namesake of the renowned composer), had been on the records for some time as a freeloader. He didn't even have an official place of residence. But since he was just a snowman, the 9th precinct police did not initiate legal proceedings against him.

Then in late February someone lodged a complaint, the gist of which was that on a nearby square, where the snowman had been spending most of his time, he'd been giving women lascivious looks. Still, out of respect for his famous namesake, the police again turned a deaf ear.

February was followed by March, and on a bright and sunny morning, the aging snowman threw all restraint to the wind and actually flung himself on a third year student from a girls' school who'd stopped on the square to admire a well-dressed shop window.

The snowman sneaked up to her, and in order to sweep the girl, who was passionate about music, off her feet, introduced himself, then in quick succession asked her to the movies, buried his nose in her hair, quarreled with her then made up, talked her into the fear of God because he was under the misapprehension that people feared God for the fun of it; then he sneaked a look inside her blouse and tried to get her to go to a buffet with him because he wanted to taste fish in aspic; then he lost his temper and called her a whore, but coming to his senses, he dropped to his knees and asked her to marry him, a proposal that, after a confused moment, the young girl to accepted.

But this just added fuel to the fire, because the oversexed snowman attempted to jumpstart their married life behind a garbage can, and the girl had to be freed of her predicament by her classmates.

At precinct headquarters, Franz Liszt was visibly contrite. But when asked the reason for his outrageous conduct, all he could say was, "Spring is in the air."

*1968*

# free will

The stewardess was thumbing through the airline schedule. She had the information at her fingertips, but she thought it best to check, just to be on the safe side.

"There's a lovely flight from Vienna arriving in Rome at 16:10 hours."

"Is that the plane that's going to explode on the runway?"

"It is," the stewardess said.

"Except, there's a problem," the passenger continued. "By the time I get to the city, the offices will be closed."

"In that case, forget Vienna, and transfer in Prague. That flight is in Rome by a quarter to one."

"That sounds better," the passenger said.

"On the other hand, there's a three hour wait in Prague," the stewardess cautioned.

"It's worth it," the passenger said. "If I take the plane out of Vienna, I lose a day."

"In that case, you're best off taking the plane out of Prague. It leaves at seven a.m. in the morning."

"That's no good," the passenger said. "If I have to get up early, I can't sleep all night."

"In short, you're losing a day either way," the stewardess acknowledged with a smile. "So then, which flight would you like to book?"

"I think I'll book the flight out of Prague after all," the passenger said, "and take a sleeping pill."

"I hope you realize," the stewardess added, "that there's a slight problem with this flight as well."

"All I know is that it will crash into a cliff in the Alps. Or is that another flight?"

"No. That's the one. It's going to be smashed to smithereens," the stewardess said, and as she handed over the ticket added, "Have a nice flight!"

# károly keleti

It's no child's play exchanging apartments these days.* If you've got well placed friends that's another matter, of course, but what has Károly Keleti got, who runs a sad little drug store in a narrow side street in a house slated for demolition?

He wasn't thinking of anything out of the ordinary, mind; his only condition was that it be located in Károly Keleti Street. But he spared no effort, left no stone unturned until he got his wish and found himself moving into a room and kitchen flat in the street of his choice.

Yet hardly had he taken a look around when he felt that something was still missing, and though the move had left him nearly destitute, he sacrificed the last of his savings, bought a name plate, and fixed it to his door. The name plate had just two words on it: Károly Keleti.

And now I have a sad tale to tell, because Károly Keleti was still not satisfied with his lot, and he had to think long and hard before he could pin down the source of his discomfort. Then he grabbed a stick of crayon and wrote Károly Keleti on the back of his winter coat.

That did the trick, though, and he's been huddled in

* Under the Communist system, apartments could not be bought but were allocated by the state. Hence, if you needed another apartment (provided you had one to begin with), you had to find someone willing to change with you.

a corner ever since, his winter coat flung over his shoulder, his face turned to the wall, his back turned to the outside world. He's even gotten married, and his wife, Mrs. Károly Keleti, has borne him two healthy baby boys. He's stopped feeling that something is still missing from his life and would like the reader to know that he and his family are hail, hardy and happy, having a grand old time of it laughing under his coat. He further challenges anyone to try and find him, if they can.

*1968*

# memoirs of a puddle

On March 22, 1972, it rained all day, and I found myself comfortably settled in front of the house at Dráva utca 7, in Budapest's 13th district, where there's a dent in the sidewalk. People kept stepping in me then cursing and berating me over their shoulder, calling me names I blush to repeat. I was a puddle for two whole days, but never once did I bristle at the insults.

Then as we know, on the 24th of the month the sun came out from behind the clouds. Oh, how paradoxical is life, to have to dry up just as the weather brightens!

What else can I say? Did I live up to expectations? Did I fail to do so? Should I have behaved differently in the dent in front of Dráva utca 7? Though it makes no difference now I'd still like to know, because there will be other puddles there after me. Our lives are short, our days numbered, and while I was down there a new generation has sprung up, potential puddles ready for action, idealistic, ambitious, and they're looking to me for an answer, nagging, wanting to know what they are to expect down there in that promising dent in the sidewalk.

But I was a puddle for just two days, and so all I can say is this: though the tone is drastic and Dráva utca is windy and the sun keeps coming out at the most inopportune of moments, at least I didn't have to flow down a sewer. Oh, what holes and dents! What bursting water mains! What potholes! It's nothing to scoff at these days! So youth of the nation, listen to me. Keep your eyes peeled on the future, and head straight for Dráva utca 7.

*1972*

# fellow citizens!

Is there anyone
out there
willing to console

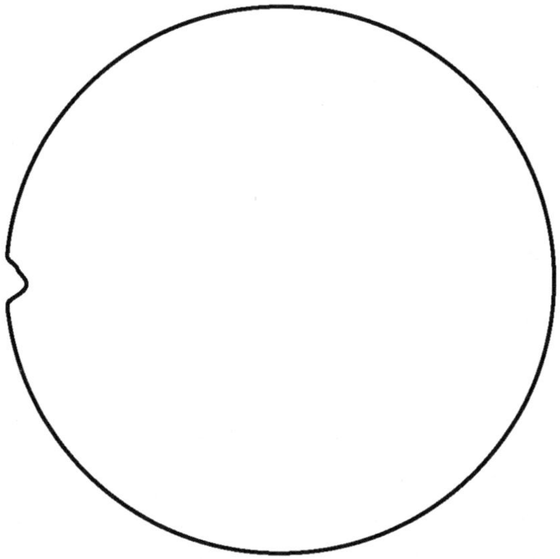

this circle
come into the world
with a slight
physical deformity?

*1969*

## birthday greetings

*for Zoltán Várkonyi's 65th birthday**

**YOUR DIFFICULTIES ARE NOW OVER**

**(p.t.o.)**

* Zoltán Várkonyi (1912–1979), renowned head of the Vígszínház, Budapest, had directed two plays by Örkény.

**YOUR DIFFICULTIES ARE JUST BEGINNING.**

*1977*

# a bright and distant future

Approximately a hundred, possibly or a hundred-and-fifteen years from now, on a bright summer's day, every church bell in the nation will ring out at the same time. Most people won't give it a second thought, whereas the chiming of the church bells will herald in a new age.

The former royal castle at Visegrád will have been rebuilt by then,* its former splendor enhanced, its halls even grander, its hanging gardens greener. At the inauguration ceremony – this is why the church bells will be ringing – some old timers will burst into tears, little wonder, considering that that will be the moment, that great and glorious moment, when the thousand year old, relentless chain of our misfortunes will have come to an end.

Visegrád will once again be the royal seat not only of this tiny country, but of the Danubian Hungarian Republic, whose shores will be washed by four or five seas.** The republic will be called Danubian in order to differentiate it from the Hungarian Republic of the Lower Rhine. The latter will not be inhabited by Hungarians though, not even then, just the people

* The royal castle of Visegrád, built around 1320, was celebrated for its beauty and grandeur. Its decline began in earnest when it fell to the Turks in 1543, which marked the beginning of Hungary's "thousand year old, relentless chain of misfortunes."

** Hungary, "in the heart of Europe", is a landlocked country.

of the Lower Rhine in their shabby clothes, who will have called themselves Magyar, hoping it would improve their luck.

If only I could describe what it will be like to be a Magyar in that bright and distant future! Let me just say that in a mere hundred-and-fifteen years, the word 'magyar' will have become a verb which will have entered every language in the civilized world – with pleasant connotations, I might add. For instance, in French, "to magyar" will mean: I am getting drunk as a skunk. In Spanish: to find money on the street and reach down for it. In Catalan: I can bend down with the greatest of ease now that the pinched nerve in my back has been miraculously cured. And should someone in London say, "I am going to magyar," it will mean: You see that gorgeous blonde over there? Well, I'm going to go up to her straight away, hook my arm through hers, take her home, and...." (Here a four letter word follows.)

Another example. In seven civilized languages (Norwegian, Greek, Bulgarian, Basque, etc.) "I magyar, you magyar, he/she/it magyars" (because the verb will be subject to proper conjugation) will mean: I am (you are, he/she/it is) eating crispy roast duck with fresh home-made cucumber salad while Yehudi Menuhin plays a csárdás in my ear.

Furthermore, in Lithuanian. "Can I go to magyar, Mom?" "Sure, magyar, if you want to," will mean that a little boy wants to go to the movies and after thinking it over, his mother gives her consent, even though the movie is not recommended for viewers under eighteen.

But never mind foreign nations! Even here at home, many things will be called by other names. For instance, 'vanilla', which is of foreign derivation, will have been replaced by 'háború' the Hungarian word for war, since it will have lost its original meaning by then. Thus, the sign above the ice cream counter at the pastry shop in Visegrád will read:

Strawberry
Punch
Háború
Chocolate.

This is what our lives will be like. All we have to do now is muddle through the next hundred-and-fifteen years as best we can.

*1967*

# notices and announcements

I hereby wish to express my infinite gratitude to all those who have graciously extended their good wishes to me on the occasion of my beloved husband's untimely death.

*

Has anyone seen my long-haired, house trained, female mid-ear infection that answers to the name of Mary?

*

We do not serve dead drunks!

*

Comradely reunion
All those who have personally participated in beating me to a pulp in the back lot of the City Park Diner are hereby cordially invited to a comradely reunion at the same place on the 20th of the month.

*The deceased B. Ordódi*

*

No littering the sidewalk with paper money!

*

Guests with male genitals kindly refrain from visiting the women's sun deck.

*

Why can't a Volkswagen find true happiness?

*

It is strictly against regulations to feed, bait, or in any way annoy the Hungarian flag!

*

Warning! The gate bites!

# asylum

In France, the equivalent of our Lipótmező is called Asile Sainte-Anne. It is a huge asylum. Its walls are as tall and sturdy as the Citadella on Gellért Hill, its grounds are twice the size of the Budapest Zoo. Its five buildings are as big as the Hungarian Parliament, and the lively bustle reminds one of a country fair.

I am busy myself, searching for Mr. and Mrs. Csikszeredai. A couple of days prior to my departure from Pest, a woman had extracted a solemn promise from me to look them up as soon as I got to Paris. She even wrote twice, reminding me of my promise. Csikszeredai and his wife had been admitted to Asile Sainte-Anne seven years previous to my visit, and there'd been no news of them since.

"We have someone here from Armenia," the young lady in the admissions office informs me. "His name is Karpeis Dorispanovich."

"That's not him," I say, and shake my head.

"What do you mean," the young lady says, wrinkling her brow.

"He's not Armenian but Hungarian, and he's not Karpeis, but Csikszeredai."

The young lady heaves a great sigh. We go through two filing cabinets. The French write the letter *'cs'* in a hundred ways. *Ts, ch, tsh.* But the Csikszeredais didn't write their name like that.

"Are you sure he's not Armenian," the young lady asks, hardly bothering to hide her annoyance.

"I'm positive," I say.

"In that case, kindly write the name down."

I write it down. She looks. Her expression brightens.

"Ah! Zhiksreday! Why didn't you say so?"

It turns out that she knows Zhiksreday very well. His mental health is satisfactory, and the previous year he was even allowed to work in the admissions office, then was sent to the countryside to engage in agricultural work on the asylum's farm. Zhiksreday was there now, too, working. His wife is a pretty young woman, if lean. She can't be more than twenty-eight, if that, and is a resident, and yes, I could see her. She's in Women's Pavilion number two. I should ask for the matron. Her name is Madame Magnan.

Madame Magnan listens patiently to what I have to say, then takes a look at the piece of paper that was shoved in my hand in the admissions office.

"Hungarian?" she asks.

"Hungarian."

"Twenty-eight years old?"

"Yes."

"In that case, I know who she is. There's only one Hungarian woman in the pavilion. Take a seat. I'll get her for you."

She leaves me in the office with five or six women who are busy typing, fiddling with their erasers, or combing their hair, and they are all looking at me. They must be patients, because they're in white coats and ankle-length white bottoms. I notice a bunch of purple flowers standing on a desk in a pickle jar. They're called snapdragons. Maybe they're mad, too, and had been brought here from a florist's where their resemblance to flowers was a source of embarrassment. I am just studying the snapdragons with a look of pity when Madame Magnan returns with a woman in a white smock bringing up the rear. She is incredibly obese and at least forty years of age. Of course, she might think she's twenty-eight, I say to myself, stand up, go to her, and bow. "How do you do, Madame," I say. "I hope you don't mind this intrusion, but Mrs. H. from the Foreign Ministry sent me with a message from your family."

At first she doesn't pay much heed. But with time a smile appears on her face and she says, "lambada". Maybe it's not lambada, but grandpapa, I can't be sure. In any case, it made no sense.

I look around, and in my confusion give her another bow. "Your family," I say, "are fine, thank God. Last week Miklós was promoted to lieutenant-colonel."

Hearing this, she becomes quite animated, explaining something urgently and at length, except I don't understand what she is saying. I go over to Madame and whisper in her ear that this lady is not Mrs. Csikszeredai.

"Well then, who is she?" Madame asks.

"I don't know," I say, "but she's not Hungarian."

"What makes you think that," Madame shrugs.

"Because I don't understand what she is saying," I explain.

"That's impossible," Madame says, giving me one of those looks, "when you had such a nice chat just now."

"Is there no other Hungarian in the pavilion?" I ask.

"She's the only one," Madame shoots back.

I decided not to stretch my luck. I bowed and headed for the door, but I could feel Madame's piercing glance on my back. Clearly, she had her suspicions about me. I cut across the park as quickly as I could, but stopped short of the gate. What's the rush, I asked myself, it can't be half bad. It must be wonderful, in fact, light and sweet, like early childhood, like ecstasy, like happiness. A man, while he is young and strong, should strive for clarity. But once he's run out of steam, it's enough if he says, "lambada". I'd go on writing for another ten years, I thought. Then I'd come back to this place, offer myself up to Saint Anne's protection, and if I should get visitors I'd say to them "lambada" and pin purple snapdragons in my hair, provided I will still have any.

*1948*

# information

He's been sitting by the main gate behind a small sliding glass window for the past eleven years, and in all that time, people have asked him only one of two questions.

"Which way to the Montex office?"

And he said:

"First floor, to the left."

The second question is:

"Where can I find Gum Residue Recycling?"

To which he replied:

"Second floor, second door to the right."

For eleven years, he has never made a mistake and everyone was given proper instructions. But one time a lady walked up to the sliding window and asked him one of the usual two questions:

"Can you tell me please where I can find the Montex office?"

But this time, quite exceptionally, he gazed into the far distance and said:

"We all come from nothing, and to a great big fucking nothing shall we return."

The lady lodged a complain with the management. The complaint was investigated, debated, then dropped.

After all, it was no big deal.

*1967*

# tulip in crisis

It came as quite a shock. It never complained. It was in the best of health. Its bulb had just yielded flowers for the seventh year in a row. It stood in full bloom on the windowsill of an elderly couple, both of whom were retired teachers. The night before it had thoroughly fertilized its pistils, after which it had a good night's sleep. But at five in the morning – flowers are notoriously early risers – it flung itself down into the street below from the fourth story window.

At first the police speculated that someone had pushed it with intent to kill. They questioned the retired teachers, but they denied the charges. They insisted that they watered it regularly, loved it, and shed profuse tears over its untimely death. The lieutenant-colonel living below them substantiated their testimony, and in a matter of days, the charges against the elderly couple were dropped.

The suicide-bent tulip was purple and introverted by nature. According to the people in the neighborhood, it lived a secluded life, so it couldn't have suffered from despair or disillusionment. Why, then, would it want to throw its life away?

The answer came one week later, when the lieutenant-colonel's wife, who was doing her spring cleaning, found the tulip's farewell note on the her balcony. She took it upstairs to the fourth floor, where the old man read the garbled lines out loud.

"When you read this note, I will no longer be among the

living. Dear sir, dear Aunt Irma, please forgive me. I couldn't help it. I didn't want to be a tulip any more."

"What could it have wanted to be, poor thing," Aunt Irma asked.

"It didn't say," her husband answered.

"A tulip," Aunt Irma said with a shake of her head. "The very idea!"

*1967*

# who is the sinner?

The judge presiding over the trial bagged a handsome stag in the animal reserve at Gyula. After he'd delivered the coup de grâce to the dying animal, he announced, "Hunting is the noblest sport there is."

The attorney for the defense was an avid butterfly collector. He pierced their abdomen with a pin and once, amidst the frantic beating of their wings, they were dead, he reflected, "Such is the thirst for knowledge."

The writer of these lines, who was the reporter at the trial, is an enthusiastic water polo fan. When a member of the team kicks his opponent in the groin under water, he cheers him on from the bleachers. "Water polo is a tough sport," he reasons.

And what did the murderer say?

He freely confessed that he'd murdered his wife, who'd cheated on him right and left, taught their daughter to be no better than she ought, and brought disaster on the entire family. With head bowed in contrition he said, "I have sinned."

And so he was hanged by due process of the law.

# our wildest dreams can come true

"Feri have you noticed? The third dog isn't pulling."

"My whip can't reach him."

"In fact, it looks to me like he's limping."

"Of course he's limping. He's got only three legs!"

"Isn't it ill advised to put a three-legged dog at the head of the team?"

"Have another look. All twelve dogs are three-legged."

"Poor things. I feel so sorry for them!"

"You should be feeling sorry for *me*. Have you any idea how hard it was to find twelve three-legged dogs?"

"I'm no expert, but I'd have thought that a normal dog would pull this thing better."

"Of course it would. But I'm a city boy. What would I do with twelve four-legged dogs?"

"Are you afraid of them?"

"I'm even afraid of a mosquito. Nature must be treated with due respect. Let's assume, just for the sake of argument, that these dogs have four legs. Let's further assume that something suddenly drives them mad and they tear the reins from my hand... But it's best not even to consider that."

"I still don't get it. If you're afraid of dogs, why do you have them pull your car?"

"Because I'm a bad driver."

"With a bit of practice you'd improve."

"To a degree. But man and automobile are not equal partners."

"Look around us. We're the only car being pulled by a team of dogs!"

"So much the worse for the other cars! Man can't keep pace with technology, no matter how hard he tries. He uses it, but deep down, he's terrified."

"I'm not afraid of cars at all."

"But this Simca can do a hundred and fifty kilometers an hour!"

"I love speeding cars. Please. Couldn't we go faster?"

"Why are you so impatient? We left Pest just ten days ago, and we're already in Siófok."*

"Considering the twelve dogs, that's not such a big deal."

"Oh, yes, it is. I pulled in the hand break before we set off."

"Aren't you overly cautious?"

"This is the speed we were created for."

"But everybody's staring at us!"

"Of course they're staring. They're jealous."

"Their eyes are popping out of their heads!"

"No wonder, when they see that even our wildest dreams can come true."

*1966*

* Siófok, near the tip of Lake Balaton, was at one time the favorite destination for vacationing Hungarians. It lies just 106 kilometers (appr. 43 miles) from Budapest.

# gravepost

**D**
**o**
**n**
**'**
**t**

**b**
**e**

**AFRAID**

**o**
**f**

**t**
**h**
**e**

dark because what so often
fills you with fear and trepidation is just
the reposeful eternity of your dreams
and the metamorphosis of the once and former molecules
of your body into cell tissue of another kind

# the meaning of life

If we string up a bunch of red hot peppers, we will end up with a wreath of red hot peppers. On the other hand, if we do not string up a bunch of red hot peppers, we will not end up with a wreath of red hot peppers. The peppers will be just as many, just as red, just as hot, but they will not be a wreath of red hot peppers.

Is it the string? No, it's not the string. The string, as we know, is a third-rate factor of little importance. What then?

Whoever falls to thinking about this and makes sure not to let his thoughts stray from the true path may come to discover many great truths.

*1967*

# thoughts from the cellar

The ball flew through a broken window and landed in the cellar. One of the children, the fourteen-year-old daughter of the concierge, hobbled down after it. A tram had cut off one of her legs, poor thing, and so she was quite happy if she could at least pick up the ball after her playmates.

The cellar was in semi-darkness, but she thought she could see something stirring in a corner.

"Kitty!" the wooden-legged daughter of the concierge called out. "What are you doing down here, dear little kitty?"

She then picked up the ball and hurried off with it as fast as she could.

The old, ugly and foul-smelling rat – for it was a rat that had been taken for a kitten – was stunned. No one had ever talked to it like that before. Up till then everyone had been repulsed by it, pelted it with bits of coal, or fled screaming for their lives. But now, for the first time, it thought how different everything would have been if only it'd been born a kitten, or better yet – because we're all insatiable, and it too continued to weave the web of its reveries – it thought how very wonderful it would have been if only it'd been born the lame daughter of a concierge. But this thought was so very beautiful, the rat couldn't even imagine it in earnest.

# spectacular christmas sale

LATEST OFFERS
FROM OUR WATCH AND JEWELRY DEPARTMENT

WATERPROOF WRIST WATCH
Works perfectly in steam and water, even
at a depth of 500 meters. Always on time, elegant, reliable!
The ideal gift for your drowned relatives!

18-STONE WATCH, MOVES IN REVERSE
Novelty!
Not only do the arms move in reverse,
but the numbering on the face
is reversed as well. (XII, XI, X, etc.),
thereby making
its owner younger by the hour!

THE SAME, WITH BUILT-IN ALARM
Also works in reverse.
If you set your alarm for six in the morning,
the clock will wake you at six
the previous morning.

## RESTORE YOUR USED BELONGINGS

### SPECIAL ONE DAY OFFER

Re-freezable snow from last year
Pre-consumed chocolate (with nuts)
Cheap! Handsome! Tasty!

## HOUSE PETS, GOLD FISH, SONG BIRDS

Buy our friendly, undemanding and faithful
*house flies*
and spare yourself the expense of keeping a dog.
Our house flies
are trained with the latest available methods.
They are only three months old, but they can already speak
fly language, and will learn the language
of their owners in just three weeks.
Entertain your guests by hiding and having your fly
call your name as it circles round the room.
Remember:
a fly in the house is worth two in the bush!

## TOY DEPARTMENT

*magicians kits*
Magic tricks to ensure hours of fun!
Four complete sets!
With a bit of practice, you too can entertain
your Christmas guests!

*1. The disappearing rabbit*
Tame white rabbit used by magicians with both animals
(the visible as well as the invisible) sold in one cage.

*2. Indian bed of nails*
Comfortable neo-baroque bed with long nails
instead of traditional springs. When the magician lies down
on it, the nails pierce his body. (Takes some getting used to.)

*3. Sword-swallowing set*
Digestible swords
with interchangeable handles, in two flavors,
chocolate & strawberry.

*4. The lady sawn in half*
A spectacular number guaranteed to bring applause.
We sell the lady who is dressed in sequined tights
in two pieces so that the magician
need not bother with sewing her in half himself.

SPECTACULAR OFFER
FROM OUR MORTUARY DEPARTMENT
*reusable funerary urn*

Black plastic urn supplied with the monograms
of the deceased in silver with holes like a salt shaker.
The holes are not on top but on the bottom,
thereby insuring that the ashes will soon empty out,
which has a double advantage:

1. With a quick change of monograms, the urn is reusable;
2. The living will be relieved of mourning, sadness, self-accusation and other unpleasant states of mind much faster.

Widows! Orphans! Soon to be deceased!
Buy your urns now!

BOOKS AND RECORDS DEPARTMENT

You can now stop reading!
Be well informed and up to date without ruining your eyes
or taxing your mind. Just buy our exclusive set
of world classics concentrated into
a *suppository.*
Proust, Kafka, Joyce and other hard to read authors
get absorbed
through the large intestines in just twenty minutes.
Hungarian invention!

*The complete works of Balzac*
Six suppositories made of pure cocoa butter
in a tasteful gift box, sold exclusively in our shop!

*1968*

## who writes the one minute stories? you or I?

### HUMANITARIANISM, 1975
### cruelty to animals

1. All manner of cruelty, stabbing, burning, binding.
2. Rough handling, baiting, beating, scaring.
3. Putting sick animals to work, making animals labor beyond their endurance; neglecting to feed, water, or see to sick animals.
4. Chasing sick animals away, beating them to death, hanging them.
5. Neglecting to have a qualified physician put down senselessly suffering or terminally ill animals.
6. Subjecting animals to painful or cruel training in order to make them perform spectacles.
7. Transporting animals under overcrowded conditions.
8. Slaughtering without sedation.

*(Rules of the Society for the Protection of Animals)*

### crimes committed by human beings against other human beings

| | |
|---|---|
| Total: | 26,742 |
| Of these: | |
| Murder | 116 |
| Attempted murder | 213 |
| Physical violence | 6,940 |
| Causing injury in the workplace | 450 |
| Traffic violations | 14,612 |

| | |
|---|---|
| Assault and battery | 3,156 |
| Aggression against officials | 1,255 |

*(Statistical Yearbook, 1975)*

## SAFE HAVEN

Height above sea level of Budapest's public buildings:
Insane Asylum at Lipótmező 215 meters

*(Budapest from 1873 to Today)*

## LETTER FROM THE EDITOR

*Endre Kárász, Eger.* The architect whose works you were "studying with approval" did not usurp the name of the Communist martyr László Rajk. He is his son.

## EMBARRASSED CHINESE

Protests against Chinese intervention in Vietnam, which is posing a serious threat to world peace, are continuing nationwide. Employees of the Offset and Playing Card Printing Works have sent a telegram of protest to the heads of the Peking government, while doctors from the National Rheumatism and Physiotherapy Institute have called for an ad hoc meeting to protest Chinese aggression.

*(Esti Hírlap, February 21, 1979)*

## SEE THE WORLD!

*Don't forget!*
*Personal experience gained while traveling*
*is worth a semester of geography and history lessons!*

Take advantage of our current one day offerings:

| | | |
|---|---|---|
| January 14: | Eger, goulash party | 185 Fts. |
| January 21: | Tök, goulash party | 230 Fts. |
| February 11: | Zebegény, goulash party | 143 Fts. |
| February 25: | Eger, goulash party | 282 Fts. |
| March 4: | Tök, goulash party | 230 Fts. |
| March 11: | Zebegény, goulash party | 143 Fts. |
| March 18: | Esztergom, goulash party | 185 Fts. |
| March 25: | Tök, goulash party | 230 Fts. |

Visit your nearest Volántourist office today!

*(Advertisement, Népszabadság, Jan. 4, 1979)*

## ABSURD HERITAGE

The exhibition planned in honor of the anniversary of Picasso's death has been postponed. The show, which was to include a selection of 44 paintings found in the artist's studio at the time of his death, was canceled when experts ascertained that several of the masterpieces were fakes.

*(Le Monde, 1977)*

## AVANTGARDE, 1836

*Note:* If I were to write this novel in France, the Prologue and Epilogue would not be included. But here at home, it is not yet time for such daring. Accordingly, those of my readers who are versed in foreign Romance literature, especially English and French, may safely leave the Prologue and Epilogue unread.

*(Miklós Jósika, Wanton People, Epilogue.)*

## ALREADY IN HUNGARIAN

1.

The masked ball held at the Seven Electors Inn was especially lively. The band from the Bentheim Armed Regiment heightened the mood by playing Lanner's most popular waltz, the *Frohsinn*, as well as a round of stylish polkas. Four masqueraders who attended in ornate Eastern costumes as well as two ladies are worthy of special attention, insofar as they conversed in Hungarian.

*(News item, January 28, 1834)*

2.

I will admit that the two of us, Baron Stephan Hauer and myself, took several lessons in executing the csárdás, *um uns populär zu machen*, and learned the steps with relative ease; but then, just a couple of days before we *in einem Volksfest auftreten und uns produciren wollten*, a certain Englishman happened to be traversing Austria, who had come to that place direct from Calcutta. We decided to surprise him with the Hungarian dance so that he could take the news with him to England, to wit, *"wie sehr vielseitig wir sind"* and extended a cordial invitation to him for tea, which he heartily accepted, and couldn't express his surprise enough in his measured, honeyed tones, feeling as if his ears were being assaulted by the death throes of a dying nation! *Um ihn aufzuheitern* we asked the band to start up the "flour miller" and we ourselves launched into the "sawing dance", and were thus able to draw the Englishman out of his profound and melancholy censure, because as soon as he set eyes on us, he burst into such hearty laughter, he could hardly catch his breath.

*Sept. 9th, 1857 (István Szécsényi, Diary)*

## ANECDOTE

Los Alamos (U.S.A.)
"Gentlemen," Einstein said turning to Leo Szilárd, John Neumann, Eugene Wigner and Ede Teller as he left the room, "you may now continue the debate in Hungarian."

## slaughterhouse

We were first guided to an observation tower, from where we could take in the full panorama. Next we admired the Renaissance court of the presidential palace. Then we visited a mineral spring where – encouraged by our guide – we tasted the sour but medicinal waters of the well. We got in the coach again, and the loudspeaker praised the beauty of the Inner City. We also stopped at the National Gallery. I looked at the sculpture collection, but I was soon in such pain, I stayed behind and did not get to see the beautiful Rembrandts and Breughels with the rest of the group.

"And now," the loudspeaker announced, "we will visit the slaughterhouse, one of the capital city's most modern institutions. The slaughter of the animals proceeds according to such humane, I might even say noble principles, that ladies with weak nerves and children too can watch without anxiety."

We passed along huge halls where everything was bathed in light. Soft music reverberated between the marble walls, with not a bellow or grunt to disturb the peace. As our path led from the weighing station to the ham smoking and tenderizing station, everything was different from what I had imagined. I did not see animals frozen with fear or grunting and squealing with terror, nor did I spot any young muscular butchers bearing down with their heavy axes. The beef-cattle, the hogs, the sheep were herded past snow-white corridors into a huge room, where they gradually turned drowsy, lay down, and passed on as smoothly as a boat would glide over an isthmus into still waters.

I pulled our guide aside.

"I have a favor to ask," I said.

"It's out of the question," she said.

"I have my reasons," I said.

"So do we all," she said.

"I wouldn't be ungrateful," I said.

"I've been offered fortunes," she said.

"Why is it just the sheep?" I said.

"I'm sorry, but it is strictly against the rules," she said.

# immortality

It was not young any more, but it still commanded respect; the inhabitants of the marshland knew and feared it, all four-legged creatures, near and far. Its eyes retained their former sharpness, and if it spotted its prey at a height of a thousand meters, it came swooping down on it like the sure blow of a sledge-hammer.

But then, in the prime of life, between two leisurely beatings of its wing, its heart stopped. Still, they did not come out of hiding – neither the rabbits, nor the gophers, nor the poultry of the nearby villages – because it was still floating up above, at a height of a thousand meters, surviving death with outstretched wings, a threatening immobility, which lasted for yet another two or three minutes, until the wind let up.

# we're an equestrian nation

A motorcycle stalls at a railroad crossing with a long line of impatient cars and carts coming up the rear. They can't pass it because a military convoy as long as my arm is approaching opposite from the direction of Füred.

The passengers of the motorcycle are a family of peasants. The father is about forty years of age. He is swarthy and squat, square faced, and is wearing black boot pants and a snow white shirt under a black overcoat. They must be on their way to a visit, because the mother, who is sitting behind him, is also wearing her Sunday best, while their young daughter with the two blonde braids perched on the sidecar is all starched ruffles, laces, and tulles. The earrings in her ears are set with light blue lapis lazuli stones the size of poppy seeds.

The man tries to jump start the motorcycle again. It burs, lurches, falters.

"Why can't you behave? Why can't you do as you're told?" the man shouts at the machine. He is clearly very angry.

He tries jump starting the motorcycle a few more times, dismounts, circles around it, then kicks in the starter again.

"May the devil take you," he yells, cursing the 250 cubic centimeter Csepel motorcycle, "and your brood, too, while he's at it!"

He squats and fidgets with the machine. He jump starts it again, and this time the motor gives a steady roar. He brushes off the knees of his pants and mounts the saddle.

Taking its sweet time, the motorcycle rolls across the railway tracks. The man's wife pulls on her rubber-rimmed safety goggles. The couple sit up straight and proud, chins held high, as if they were great lords in a padded coach. The man grips the handlebars. His wrists are loose and his elbows are pointed straight out, the way it has always been since man came to be put on this earth along with the horse, and horse equipment, too.

*1956*

# gli ungheresi

Ice cream was originally invented by Ugo Riccardo Salvatore Giulio Girolamo B., a baker from Catania. The precise date is still an object of debate, so let's not worry about it; it was more or less at the same time as the invention of the printing press.

Besides inventing ice cream, Ugo also invented a thin waffle cone to go with it, plus a push cart. (Which is just as it should be. It's inconceivable that Irinyi, for instance, should have invented the match, leaving the match box to someone else, or that Ehrlich should have discovered Salvarsan, and someone else syphilis. That would be absurd.) Anyway, after he had perfected his invention in this manner, Ugo decided to go public with it.

He traveled through Lodomeria and Bessarabia, Tirol, Burgundy, Brandenburg, and even the Wendish captaincy. One can imagine the reception he got, but one cannot describe it adequately. Wherever he appeared with his small cart, young and old gathered round him clutching their money in their hands and smacking their lips as, with flutterig hearts, they waited for their raspberry, strawberry, chocolate, lemon, and pistachio ice cream. Ugo gave everyone what they asked for, and in order to save them unnecessary experimentation, he even told them that all they have to do was lick the ice cream. Wherever he went he was greeted with glee, and when it was time for him to move on, the people were much saddened, and hoped for his swift return.

One time, Ugo even visited Hungary. (Italian: *Ungheria.*) But in Hungary the king had just instituted a new tax on salt, and so young and old could talk about nothing else except the new salt tax. His vanity hurt and himself desperate, Ugo attached a bell to his push cart and, with more eagerness than usual, showed his ice cream to the few that gathered around him. However, the Hungarians (Italian: *gli ungheresi*) couldn't have cared less. They didn't feel the heat of the summer, and so had no need of anything to cool them down; their heads were too full with the new tax on salt. Though Ugo tried to explain to them that they could go on thinking whatever they wanted, because all they had to do was lick his ice cream, they said thank you but no thank you, we've got more than enough to lick already.

But, Ugo protested, having been mortally wounded by such cruel indifference, each one of his ice creams has a different taste! So what, the mule-headed Hungarians shot back, all they have to do is suck on their five fingers, each one has a different taste, too. And when Ugo would still not relent, they bombarded him with horse manure, thinking that in his hodge-podge of a language, *gelatti* (Hungarian: *fagylalt*) must mean, "Long live the tax levied on salt!" Needless to say, they couldn't very well put up with that.

Broken in mind and body, poor Ugo managed to push his cart as far as the duchy of Zára, but from there he had to be taken home by boat. On his deathbed, where he was surrounded by the ice cream vendors of Italy, he was heard to repeat just two words, over and over, *"Gli ungheresi... gli ungheresi,"* then he gave up the ghost.

# encounter

Since the city council allows only 40 watt bulbs in the stairwells of Budapest's apartment houses, the lighting is far from adequate, to say the least. As soon as it gets dark everything is blurred and indistinct, and you can't even tell if the person coming towards you is a male or a female.

This poor lighting may have been partly responsible for the fact that a tenant, Attila Markstein, the outstanding Bach pianist who was humming a pleasant fugue to himself on the stairwell just then, couldn't decide whether he was on the first or the second floor, and so began running up and down the stairs simultaneously, as a result of which he bumped into himself on the first-floor landing.

He did not lose his composure, though. He knew that it could not be schyzophrenia, because it wasn't his psyche but his body that had doubled. He let out a cry, but only because on his way down he'd kicked himself in the shin, while on his way up he butted himself in the stomach.

"I'm sorry," he said in his celebrated good manners. "It's entirely my fault."

"Not in the least. I saw you coming up the stairs and making a turn on the landing."

"It must have been too late."

"I had plenty of time to slow my pace," the Markstein who was standing further up said with a wave of the arm. "But instead of going round you, I spit in your face."

"Ah, but surely, it wasn't intentional," his much surprised

timid self remarked. "It must have happened because I butted you in the stomach on my way up."

"Still, that was no reason for me to pull a knife."

"But I saw how short tempered you are, so I wiped the spit off and wrung the knife from your hand."

"Is that what you call being short tempered?" the Markstein that was standing further up said sarcastically. "Each of my four grandparents were alcoholics. The descendants of alcoholics have a seventy per cent chance of inheriting criminal tendencies."

"Spitting someone in the face is hardly criminal. It's my fault for not having apologized."

"Don't play the martyr with me, Markstein. If provoked, I could slam a newborn babe against the wall."

"Good Lord! It's people like you who end up causing fascism!"

"Also, I make advances to my elderly mother," one Markstein said to the other Markstein with a grin. "You, on the other hand, wouldn't know Oedipus from a platypus!"

"It's the first I've heard the word, to be sure."

"All the same, it's high time you accepted the fact that I'm the monster living inside you. And now, good bye."

What's to be done in a situation like this? Take it in stride. Which, of course, is not easy, especially for a man who – or so Markstein reasoned – had been completely at one with himself all his life. He was so thoroughly at one with himself, you couldn't have dropped a pin and have it land. But truth is relentless, while man is not wholly resistant, so however reluctantly, Attila Markstein learned to live with himself.

But Markstein was in for another surprise when on the following Tuesday he (both of them) woke to the sound of singing. Imagine Markstein's shock when he found that he was the one doing the singing! And what was he singing? Well? Bach? No. Not even Buxtehude. Guitar in hand, he was belting out the following silly, overly sentimental melody painful to his refined ear:

*The old home town looks the same*
*As I step down from the train*
*And there to meet me is my mama and my papa*
*Down the road I look and there runs Ma…*

He jumped to his feet. Is that him, too? And if it is, how many more Attila Marksteins might be waiting to make their appearance? And if they do, what then? How far can a cover of skin stretch? Surely, it must have its limits. How many more Attila Marksteins could he safely accommodate?

*1968*

## bad dream

The welder Kálmán Kirch reached home at three o'clock at night. He paid the cabbie, then rang the front door bell.* The concierge didn't answer. He scooped up some snow and pressed it to his forehead. He had too much to drink and needed to cool down. He rang again.

The snore that was next in line to erupt in the concierge's throat never made it, and the bitter taste of ire scalded the roof of his mouth. He hated people in general, but he hated the tenants, most especially the welder, who was always late coming home, in particular. In his prayers he often prayed for some calamity to befall him. He was an avid prayer, because he belonged to a sect that didn't believe in anything except the Gospels and celebrated Saturday instead of Sunday.

Kirch knew nothing about the wild passions stirring inside the concierge's breast. He worked the afternoon shift on Elizabeth Bridge. When he finished work, he went to a foul smelling place with music and drank three double shots of Szatmári brandy. After three double shots of Szatmári brandy, you love your fellow men. So when the concierge finally came to the front door, Kirch hooted:

"Good evening, dear sweet Mr. Hornák."

* Until the late 1970s, the front doors of apartment houses were locked at 10 p.m., and the only key was with the dreaded concierge – an expedient way to spy on the late-night activities of tenants and their visitors.

"Go to hell, you filthy, foul smelling pig," the concierge grumbled, but not too loud, so it could be taken for a greeting of sorts.

If anybody rang him before midnight, he managed to go back to sleep. Luckily, in the newest houses of the newest housing projects, like his, the tenants were early risers – physical laborers and clerks. Only this drunken pig woke him up in the middle of the night, when he couldn't go back to sleep any more, just toss and turn in bed. He grumbled into his pillow, as if singing a lullaby, "Go to hell, snotty, blond pig, go to hell!"

Kirch sent the elevator back down, walked into his apartment, and changed into his pajamas. He was always a touch giddy. It took twelve welders to dismantle the bridge in three shifts. Anybody watching them from below got the shivers, so they were paid as much as the wage ceiling permitted. But up there, in the deep of the night, they did not feel the danger. They did not feel the vertiginous depth below them, just the starry sky above. Their blue working light lit up the city. They could have welded the earth to the sky, of only they wished. Women got goose bumps when they learned where he worked, and Kirch liked that, too. He always did what he liked, and doing what he liked would invariably make him feel a bit giddy.

He opened the balcony door. He stepped out on the balcony. He took a deep breath. He yawned. The air smelled of snow and plaster, and the snow and the plaster also smelled, just a bit, of Szatmári plumb brandy. This medley of smells made Kirch's head reel, so he took another step forward.

He was standing in air. The balcony rails were not yet up. There was a slip by the main entrance saying, "It is strictly forbidden to step out on the balcony," and Kirch read the slip every day, but he didn't interiorize its contents, because he entertained a deep seated antipathy for anything being forbidden. He took only what he liked seriously, and since he liked the light winter breeze, he took yet another step forward. And then another. And then down he plunged, two stories, plus the mezzanine. Kirch plunged downward for some time, and he liked that, too. As the wind blew through his pajamas, he felt naked. He did a salto, then fell into a mound of snow. The snow crawled up his pajama legs. Kirch was ticklish. He laughed. Then he climbed out, brushed the snow off his legs, and rang the front doorbell again.

Mr. Hornák was startled, but he continued to lie flat, staring into the dark. At first he was angry, thinking that it might be the welder, but his anger subsided as quickly as it had come when he remembered that the drunken pig was at home upstairs. He climbed out of bed. He pulled a pair of pants over his nightshirt, and his winter coat over that, and a scarf over that. He shuffled out to the front door. When he reached the door, his eyes popped out of his head, a cold shiver ran down his spine, and the blood froze in his veins.

"Good evening, dear sweet Mr. Hornák," the welder hooted, then got in the elevator.

Because of the dull background throb of the elevator, he couldn't hear Mr. Hornák outside screaming inarticulately as he ripped off his scarf, his winter coat, his pants, his nightshirt. The paramedics wrapped him in a blanket and rushed him to the psychiatric clinic where, even as he fell into a deep slumber, he thrashed about violently, gritting his teeth. As these lines are being written, he is still in a state of mental collapse.

# one wednesday morning

When the alarm clock went off at 6 a.m. one Wednesday morning, Frigyes Haller did not wake up.

Mrs. Haller went to the kitchen to put up the coffee, calling to her husband in the meantime. Then she brought him his coffee, still calling to him, berating him, shaking him. But Haller still did not wake up. Twenty minutes later, the paramedic told Mrs. Haller that her husband was gone. The cause of death: cardiac arrest.

Mrs. Haller just sat there, sobbing uncontrollably. She didn't even have the presence of mind to inform her neighbors. At nine-thirty she tied a black kerchief around her head and went to work. On the way, she sent her son a telegram – he was living in Hamburg – and another to her daughter, who was married in a small town and was just expecting the birth of her baby. In both cases, the message was the same: "Your father is gone. His heart stopped beating."

Her co-workers – because Mrs. Haller headed straight for the machine shop – were struck dumb. If they hadn't seen Mrs. Haller with her cried-out eyes, they might not have believed it. Frici, dead? Impossible! Why, just the other day he was fit as a fiddle. He was his old quiet self, he smoked a lot, and was the last in the showers, because he liked to wash up when no one else was around. No. Such a thing was out of the question.

To make matters worse, Mrs. Haller reproached herself for having been too loud, even rude, when she turned on her husband because he, poor man, refused to wake up. The supervisor's head reeled, because he'd known Haller the best and for the longest time. He made Mrs. Haller a cup of coffee. He'd have liked to tell her that it's no use torturing herself, because it made no difference to her husband any more, but he couldn't get a word out. He just stood there with the cup of coffee until at long last he pressed it in Mrs. Haller's hand.

Very little work was done in the machine shop that day. The people just stood around, walking hither and thither, trying to guess the cause of death, and more to the point, what makes a heart stop? They recounted all sorts of stories, both old and new, that had little or nothing to do with Haller's case, but which happened in the machine shop where he'd been with them until the previous day. This is how the workday passed. But the hours, as they dragged on, brought no relief. The people went home puzzled, angry, staring morosely into space, and even at home, they could talk about nothing else. It's all they could think of.

Haller had been working in the factory for twenty-two years, always on the same of machine, because whenever a new machine was brought in, one was invariably given to him, he was so adroit with his hands. And so, before long, someone had tacked a notice on the workshop bulletin board with a picture of him framed in black and a touching, lyrical eulogy to say a last goodbye "to our unforgettable Frigyes Haller, our beloved Uncle Frici, an old and stalwart member of our factory, whose heart stopped beating."

Generally, these bulletins don't attract much attention, but someone must have noticed the picture and the news and must have been struck by the fact that such a long standing employee of an old and illustrious factory did not wake up one morning, and as a result – though without the picture, and the already brief biography even briefer – MTI, the official Hungarian news agency, published the news of Haller's death for all to read. A paper in the capital and one in the provinces also reported the news of Haller's death, even if in an even more abbreviated manner. What's more, quite unexpectedly, the largest Hamburg daily also published the news that F. Haller of Budapest, Hungary, died with tragic suddenness when his heart stopped beating.

The Hamburg newspaper learned about the event not from any news agency, though, but from Frigyes Haller, Jr., who was working as an air traffic controller at the city's airport, and who, when he received the telegram, translated its contents for the benefit of his colleagues, who were as shocked as he was. Since he was an employee of the company, Frigyes Haller, Jr. received a free ticket for the next flight to Budapest which, we must add, was the last to take off from a German airport, because the Lufthansa personnel organized a solidarity strike to protest the serious and irreversible stroke of bad luck that their colleague's father had suffered.

We will now cut to the chase, though not as much as you might think. Mankind is slow in recognizing the true import of events. For instance, on the evening of the day when the obituary appeared, all that could be observed – provided anyone noticed – was that fewer people attended the movies and the theater than usual, and the late-night bars were practically deserted. It took another twenty-four hours for the people of Budapest, who were otherwise highly sensitive, to realize what had really happened. What probably made them realize it was the fact that the miners – first at Tatabánya, then in the other mines – came up to the surface and refused to go back down again. Who is to guarantee, they argued, that what had happened to Frigyes Haller won't happen to them? Besides, if they take it in stride – not that such a thing can ever be taken in stride, mind you! – before you know it, hearts might stop beating all over the place.

Tatabánya (for in all fairness we must point this out) had

close ties to Frigyes Haller, whose son-in-law, a mining engineer, was working in pit number 4, and whose pregnant wife was coming to the end of her term. When the telegram came, she was just about to go into labor. The news of the death was bad enough, but that it should happen to the father of an expectant woman, well, no miner worth his salt could stand by and put up with it.

From noon, Budapest Radio played nothing but funeral music, the lamps on the streets were lit, and the government declared five days of mourning. Students at Moscow's Lomonosov University went on hunger strike, the British fleet headed for a safe harbor, and the president of the United States expressed a desire to attend Frigyes Haller's funeral in person. Eminent physicians from all four corners of the earth headed for Budapest in order to be present at the autopsy, because many people – especially in the field of science – hoped that it would provide the key to the dark, disturbing secret of Frigyes Haller's demise.

But not so the people of the world! These billions upon billions knew only that somewhere there was someone whose heart had stopped beating early one morning, and that was more than enough for them. They attached no hopes to the autopsy, and come evening, they were afraid to fall asleep, because from that day onward, they could never again be sure that they or their loved ones would wake up from their nocturnal slumber.

*1972*

# news and pseudo-news

I am a passionate newspaper reader. I love to pick up the newspaper in the morning and read it from cover to cover.

What is the object of this interest? Everything that has occurred on five continents since the day before. Millions upon millions share this interest, and there is an international network to bring us the news. This costs horrendous amounts of money. The other day, though, I realized that it could be dispensed with.

How did I come to realize this?

I spent a month abroad. After a while, I missed reading the morning's news. At the end of the second week, I found an old Budapest newspaper we'd used to wrap the hot plate. I smoothed it out and read it, then read it again the next day, and the day after that. As I was reading I suddenly realized that yesterday's news are every bit as interesting as today's.

This made me think. If old news are in no way less interesting than the latest news, it may not even matter if what I'm reading is real news or not. Possibly my curiosity can be satisfied with pseudo-news.

I tried it, and it worked. In what follows, I will make a handful of pseudo-news public, items I jotted down in a matter of hours without any effort at all. I hope that these pseudo-events will satisfy my readers' curiosity as they have mine. Now that would be big news, indeed.

## NEWS FROM FOUR CORNERS OF THE EARTH

### POPE LEARNS TO RIDE BIKE

On the advice of his physicians, the head of the Catholic Church rides around the huge court in front of St. Peter's Basilica on his bicycle three times every morning. Except for his physician, the Pope is accompanied on his rounds only by six Swiss guards wearing white crash helmets. The people of Rome, the simple tourists and pilgrims, attend the Holy Father's morning exercise on their knees.

### DEADLY FRENCH FRIES

Mrs. Lőrinc Kovács, a widow who lives in Óbuda, made herself French fries for dinner. As soon as she took one bite of the French fries, she clutched her stomach and died. The autopsy revealed that besides the French fries, the elderly widow's stomach also contained a bunch of forget-me-nots, a Kijev-type camera bought on a National Savings Bank loan, and a copy of Endre Fejes's book, *A Generation of Rust*.* Doctors believe that these extraneous objects may have also contributed to Mrs. Kovács's untimely death.

* Endre Fejes (b. 1923) wrote *A Generation of Rust* in 1962. This post-revolutionary novel raises the uncomfortable question, after years of socialist propaganda, what had the working class really gained? Its unadorned, factual language must have also been much to Örkény's liking.

## HUNGARIAN IN SPACE

According to unconfirmed reports, second pilot Captain Conrad of the American spaceship Gemini IV is of Hungarian origin. His father, whose name was Konrád, emigrated from Hungary, "the country of three million beggars", in the 30s. During his mission, Captain Conrad, who used to serve in the air force and still speaks fluent Hungarian, kept humming the old Hungarian song, "O, say, can you see, by the stars' early light," which he'd learned from his father.

## MAN EATS HIS OWN LEG

Géza Mendelényi, a clerk at the Headquarters for the Equitable Distribution of Dairy Products, chewed the flesh off his left leg in the garden of his home. When asked why he did it, his response was: too much vexation at the office.

## NEW WATERMELON SCOURGE

Mrs. B. Reme, member of the Freedom Co-operative of Kiskorpás, was stirred awake late last night by muffled groans. Mrs. Reme, who is a conscientious plant supervisor, hurried in wake of the sound to find a moaning watermelon in the co-op's vegetable patch. The watermelon was rushed to the county hospital.

When he heard that the watermelon belonged to the co-operative, chief surgeon Dr. Bodrogi called off his upcoming IBUSZ trip to Yugoslavia.* The watermelon will be undergoing

* IBUSZ was the acronym for the state travel agency that, until the 1980s, had a monopoly on foreign travel.

surgery. All lines at the hospital are busy, because the co-operatives of the region are anxious for news about its health.

### COLLECTOR OR BLACK MARKETEER?

József Szederjesi Szabó of Cleveland, who is of Hungarian origin, was fined one thousand forints for having amassed a suitcasefull of signs from various buildings in Budapest. The signs say, "Working elevator". Szabó insisted that he did not wish to sell the signs but acquired them for his own amusement, because he is an avid collector of curiosities.

### NEW PROSPECTS IN THE SPORTS INDUSTRY

Experts at the South-Transdanubian Deep Drill Company of Süttőlapocka received quite a surprise yesterday when, having reached a depth of 2,200 meters, instead of oil, a sea of tennis shoes shot up from the dig and headed straight for the sky. The quality controllers of the Duna Shoe Factory who rushed to the spot ascertained that the tennis shoes satisfy the most stringent quality requirements. It is hoped that the Süttőlapocka discovery will provide not only for the domestic market, but will also help us fulfill our contractual agreement with the Afghanistani Ministry of Foreign Trade.

### REVOLUTIONARY BUZZ IN PARAGUAY

Dissatisfied with their hire, the 3rd armored tank division stormed the Presidential Palace in the Paraguayan capital of Asuncion. After some light shooting, they ousted Lopez Burillo, the reactionary right wing America party president and installed the liberal-thinking Aurelio Lapaz in his place. Just as our paper went to press, the population of the city started gathering for a torchlight parade in celebration of the latest triumph of liberalism.

MORE REVOLUTIONARY BUZZ IN PARAGUAY

Dissatisfied with their hire, the air force dropped a paratrooper division into the courtyard of the Presidential Palace in the Paraguayan capital of Asuncion. After some light shooting, they ousted Aurelio Lapaz, the reactionary right wing American party president who'd spent only forty-five minutes in office. The new president, the liberal-thinking Lopez Burillo, is being cheered by the populace of the city who have gathered for a torchlight parade in celebration of the latest triumph of liberalism. As we go to press, the parade is still going strong.

I hope the above pseudo-news will have satisfied my readers' thirst for sensation. If I succeed, it would make all the media apparatus around the world completely superfluous, from the Telstars through the news agencies, cables, and all other transporters of the latest news.

We could save huge amounts of money. We could even make the newspaper editors superfluous because in lieu of a nominal fee, the author of these lines is willing to keep the domestic press supplied with interesting, up to the minute, completely authentic pseudo-news.

*1965*

# the laundress's dream

When János Baliskó left his office, he got on a streetcar and headed straight for the Inner City. After reading in the papers four months before that they'd be throwing thirteen-thousand small size washing machines on the market, Baliskó was all aflutter. He'd been pinning hundred-forint bills together with a stickpin, hiding the slowly but steadily growing pile in an obscure corner of his home, so the women wouldn't find it. He now made the last one hundred meters from the stop to the electrical appliance shop on a trot, afraid that someone might swipe the last washing machine from under his nose. The thing is, Baliskó was bent on electrifying his household.

He bundled the white enameled washing machine in a cab and took it home to Nagy Lajos Király utca.

The washing machine set him back nearly a month's salary. He and his wife were both working, and though they weren't making very much money, what they earned they spent freely, because they had no children. Still, when his mother-in-law, the widow Mrs. Szievert, asked how much the washing machine had cost, Baliskó admitted to only two weeks' salary.

Lucky for him, the women didn't think he'd been extravagant. On the contrary. They were speechless with joy, afraid even to touch the tips of their fingers to the lid of the machine. It wasn't until Baliskó explained how it worked and let them peek inside its belly, that the widow Szievert venture to ask:

"Is it Hungarian?"

"Yes, it's Hungarian," Baliskó said.

"Too bad," the widow Szievert cried.

"Why do you say that, Mother?"

"Because that means it's expensive. They got you over a barrel again, son."

"What's good is never expensive, Mother," Baliskó commented.

"Who said it's good? Last time, too, the electric grinder burnt out in less than an hour."

There was no denying that the electric grinder had burnt out. But the washing machine did not. The washing machine washed. Droning, humming, playful and nimble, it washed and washed and washed, the way the wind blows or a stream trickles, without the least sign of effort or exertion. The Baliskó family set about washing with a vengeance. They washed like one possessed, or better yet, mesmerized. There was no stopping them. That night their evening meal consisted of their leftover lunch, but even so, they ate it cold, standing up, and in a hurry.

The machine washed all their dirty clothes. It gobbled up the pillow slips, it washed clean the bed sheets. At half past nine Baliskó and his wife went to bed, because they had to get up at six in the morning. The widow Szievert said she'd go up to the attic to put the clothes out on the clothesline to dry.

When she returned and stood face to face with the washing machine, she felt so fresh and energetic, all thoughts of going to bed herself were gone. She pulled up a stool and for a while gazed at the washing machine with a friendly smile. At the bottom of a cupboard she found a bundle of old, used underwear destined for patching or use as dust rags; she quickly washed them, then returned with all their kitchen towels and floor rags. Next she rang her neighbor's door bell. The Hoffmans had three children. She asked for their dirty laundry. It was a quarter past midnight when she finished with this batch as well.

Everyone was fast asleep on Nagy Lajos Király utca. Only the washing machine gave no thought to sleep, and the widow Szievert gave no thought to sleep. She brought a ladder, climbed to the top and, her heavy body swaying precariously at a considerable height, she removed the drapes from the windows and offered them up to the machine. But by a quarter past one these, too, were clean, with ne'er a dirty rag left in the apartment, so the widow Szievert trundled down to the first floor and knocked on Géza Pasa's door.

Géza Pasa was a bachelor. He worked the afternoon shift, so it took some doing before she could knock some life back into him and make him understand why the widow Szievert was at the door. But then he gathered up two bundles of dirty laundry. When the widow Szievert was finished with them as well, it was very late, indeed, and dawn was about to break. So just as she was, in her clothes and shoes, her wet apron, her hair damp from the steam, she lay down on the unmade sofa.

Hardly had she taken three winks, and she was back doing the wash. She washed her son-in-law's light raincoat, the one that, strangely enough, no one had thought of washing before. Next – though by now she had to think real hard – she washed the horrendous amount of clothes that had accumulated back in the fall when she got laid up in hospital for six weeks with arthritis. Then she remembered a lace panty she hadn't worn in a long, long time, not since Ferry Oszkár Road, in the basement of a villa, when she collapsed in a pool of blood and suffered a spontaneous abortion. She washed that spotless clean as well. Then she threw her dear departed daughter Juliska's underwear in the machine, followed by poor Uncle Szievert's shirts and underpants, the Uncle Szievert who'd been her husband and died a hero's death by the bridge at Piave. She also washed the seven delicate handkerchiefs of which Mrs. Virava had said, "Look dear, I'm not insinuating anything, but seven of my batiste handkerchiefs disappeared during the ironing." After that she no longer considered what she was washing, she just kept feeding the days, weeks, and years into the washing machine. The basements swimming in steam. The wet concrete floors. The stewed cabbage lunches. The incurable redness of her hands. The cold, perfidious, serpentine chill that slid up her calves in photo-finish with her fatigue. She dragged the baskets, the heaps, the mountains, the mounds – entire mountain chains – to the washing machine that previously she had soaked, soaped, washed and rinsed herself.

When at six in the morning her daughter and son-in-law got out of bed, the widow Szievert was panting in her sleep, with her mouth agape. She slept with such hunger, such voracious, gluttonous appetite, they didn't have the heart to wake her. They covered her with a down comforter and went to work without breakfast, because that morning there was not a drop of milk to be had anywhere in the house.

*1955*

# hidden talent

On a bright and sunny spring day, Elek Bárd, a thirty eight year old bank clerk, his wife, née Nóra Ulrich, an artiste ten years his junior, and their two children, went to the Zoo. However, when they tried to go up to the gate, their way was barred by a huge crowd, as well as a number of police cars, fire engines, and ambulances. It seemed that a fifteen meter long cobra had escaped from the reptile house and was slithering around the ticket booth.

"Excuse me," Mrs. Bárd said repeatedly as she made her way through the crowd, then walked up to the cobra. She hummed a pleasant and ingratiating tune for him, then stroked his murderous head, after which she walked through the gate. The cobra followed her obediently in, over the lawn, past the lion and tiger cages, and back to its own cage, which the artiste carefully closed, then leisurely rejoined her family.

"How did you do that?" her husband asked in the midst of the awed crowd.

"Oh, it was nothing," his wife answered, lowering her eyes. "I'm a certified snake charmer."

"Why didn't you tell me?" her husband said.

"You never asked," his wife said and then, taking her sons by the hand, the family made for the main gate.

*1961*

# honeymooners on flypaper

They made up their minds to stay home. Why leave Budapest, the brand new husband reasoned, when it's such a spectacular city? There's the theater, the movies, concerts. There's so much to see. And so, they stayed, and their honeymoon was spent in love and contentment. Then around five-thirty one afternoon, they got stuck on the flypaper hanging from the ceiling lamp. What silly nonsense!

*

| | |
|---|---|
| *The husband:* | Do you love me, kitten? |
| *The wife:* | What a question. |
| *The husband:* | Well, then, come on. |
| *The wife:* | Again? |
| *The husband:* | Come-come-come-come-come. |
| *The wife:* | Oh, you little devil! |
| *The husband:* | Come on, munchkins! |
| *The wife:* | In a moment. My heel. I think it's stuck. |
| *The husband:* | Well, kick off your shoes, bunny. Just don't keep me waiting. |
| *The wife:* | You want to stay in again tonight? They're playing Tchaikovsky at the Academy. |
| *The husband:* | To hell with Tchaikovsky. |
| *The wife:* | We could see a show. |
| *The husband:* | Never. I can't abide Hungarian directors. |

They spoon-feed their audience. Do you feel this swaying back and forth?

*The wife:* What swaying?

*The husband:* I feel like I'm hanging from something and I'm swaying back and forth in the air.

*The wife:* Well, ignore it. Look up what's playing at the Opera.

*The husband:* Where's the paper?

*The wife:* On the kitchen table.

*The husband:* I can't. My foot's stuck.

*The wife:* I think it's *The Masked Ball.*

*The husband:* Tell me something. The stuff that your shoe is stuck in. Is it a gooey, shiny substance?

*The wife:* Something like that.

*The husband:* Now my hands are stuck as well.

*The wife:* Will you stop? We'll end up sitting at home again.

*The husband:* What's this jerking motion?

*The wife:* I'm trying to pull free of this sticky mess.

*The husband:* Well, don't. You'll tear the strip.

*The wife:* How can you be so complacent? I fell in love with you because you were adventurous and you could always make me laugh, and you said how you loved music.

*The husband:* What good is music if I can't move my limbs?

*The wife:* One would think you were the first one on earth to bet stuck. Think of the handicapped. Think of those with missing limbs! They go on with their lives, don't they? They work, don't they? Now and then they even have some fun!

*The husband:* Oh, God, now we're turning round and round, I swear.

*The wife:* Will you stop complaining?

*The husband:* I can't imagine what's going on.

*The wife:* You can't? Then I'll tell you. There's a draft from the stairwell and it's making this gooey strip turn round. Well, are you satisfied?

*The husband:* Satisfied? Satisfied, when I'm stuck up to my belly in this gooey mess?

*The wife:* All you can think about is you, you, you! It's ten to seven. Now we'll have to take a cab if we're to make it to the Opera on time.

*The husband:* Don't facts ever influence you, dear?

*The wife:* I thought we said this marriage would be different. I thought we said we would never stop talking to each other. And be attentive. We wouldn't bicker, and we wouldn't get a divorce. I want to laugh and I want to have three children, and I want them to learn the piano.

*The husband:* Oh, Lord, now it's up to my lips.

*The wife:* Will you kindly call us a cab!

*1966*

# hungarian moon rocket back on earth

*interview with the two astronauts*

1.

"I'm glad to greet you here in the festooned buffet of the Kelenföld railroad station now that you've landed. It was quite a remarkable achievement."

"I'm glad to be here."

"Everyone is anxious to learn more about you. Will you tell us something about yourself?"

"There's nothing to tell. I'm just like anybody else."

"You're too modest."

"I never underestimate my abilities. Even though I have high blood pressure and suffer from a fear of heights, still, I was picked out of fifty thousand volunteers."

"How did it happen?"

"I've worked in lots of places in responsible jobs, and each place gave the committee a glowing report."

"For instance?"

"The personnel department of the 7th district Adél Frühauf Midwife Academy, which is where I worked last wrote, 'The capabilities she has acquired in midwife training will stand her in good stead in outer space.'"

"You must be exceptionally talented. You must have dreamt of flying to the moon ever since you were a child."

"As a matter of fact, I never gave it a thought."

"Well, then, what is it you like to do?"

"I like to catch gophers. Chase them out of their holes."

"Gophers? Why?"

"I don't know. Maybe because I like gopher soup."

"Well, how did you get to be picked then?"

"I have no idea. I was undergoing treatment for bleeding ulcers at St. Roch's Hospital when a delegation of scientists entered the room. 'Accept our best wishes, Comrade. You're being sent to the moon.' What could I say?"

"Well, what did you say?"

"Nothing. The gastric probe was hanging out of my mouth. I just nodded."

"I see. Now tell us something about the moon."

"The moon is a celestial body that revolves around the earth and always shows its same side towards it. Consequently, its other side cannot be seen from here."

"Did you notice anything else?"

"What was there to notice?"

"Is there, for instance, life on the moon?"

"I'm glad you asked, because I'm sure other people would like to know, too. The surface of the moon is so full of craters that I tried to wash gophers out of their holes. I even sacrificed the last of my drinking water."

"And?"

"Nothing."

"Are you saying that there are no gophers on the moon?"

"Yes."

"What a shame. Still, your safe return from such a long trip and, as I see, in the best of health, is a cause for celebration, don't you think?"

2.

"Oh! Here comes the commander! Captain, sir, can you spare a moment to talk to us?"

"Just make it snappy. I have an upset stomach."

"It must be due to the state of weightlessness."

"No. It's due to the Hungarian beef goulash."

"You took Hungarian beef goulash with you to outer space?"

"Of course not. An overly hospitable family forced it on us out there."

"Are you saying there are people on the moon? Your second in command said nothing about it."

"My second in command is an outstanding astronaut. But she's not a good observer. She doesn't care much for people. She didn't even show up for the goulash. She says she feels sorry for the animals."

"So you're saying there are people on the moon."

"Yes. And I was pleasantly surprised to learn that they are all Hungarians whom you will be pleased to hear have adapted beautifully to the extreme climatic and other local conditions. They've become both heat and cold resistant. Also, due to a lack of oxygen – because, as you know, there's no oxygen on the moon – they breath from paper bags that contain air they'd brought with them from home."

"That's very touching. But apart from the fact that they're Hungarian, what else do they do?"

"Apart from the fact that they're Hungarian? Nothing. Being Hungarian takes up all their time."

"Do they know anything about us?"

"Everything, basically, except with some delay. Due to the great distance, for example, they're just witnessing the reign of Emperor Francis Joseph II through their telescopes."

"Did you see him yourself?"

"Just for a second, as he was declaring war on Serbia. Of course, from there, objects don't have height. Francis Joseph was completely flat. Only his beard jotted out from inside of him. He looked like a one forint coin with hair."

"How interesting. Did you learn or experience anything else in outer space?"

"Oh, I saw many wonderful things."

"I'm not surprised, considering how observant you are. What was the most interesting thing you experienced?"

"I was most surprised by the fact that there's not one moon, but two."

"How do you mean? One hidden behind the other?"

"No. Of course not. They practically overlap, with just a very small space between them."

"That's remarkable. No one has ever noticed that before."

"Really? In that case, I must have been mistaken."

*1968*

# historical mistake

"Hello? Moloko?"
"Excuse me?"
"Moloko?"
*"Vy po-russki govorite?"*[*]
"I'm sorry. I don't understand."
"Well, neither do I, madame."
"I want to speak to my son-in-law."
"In that case, why did you ask for moloko?"
"Why not?"
"Because it's Russian for milk."
"But that's what I call my son-in-law."
"Well, that's not me."
"But I'm sure I dialed the right number."
"In that case, there must be some grave mistake, madame."

* Do you speak Russian?" The short piece is a reference to the absurdity of the Russians "calling" on the Hungarians when they marched into the country in 1945 and forgetting to leave. A historical mistake, if ever there was one.

# the quick and effective clearing up of an embarrassing historical mistake*

"Hello? Moloko?"

"Excuse me?"

"Moloko?"

"Vy po-russki govorite?"**

"I'm sorry. I don't understand."

"Well, and I don't understand you, madame."

"I want to speak to my son-in-law."

"In that case, why did you ask for moloko?"

"Why not?"

"Because it's Russian for milk. Or is that his name?"

"It's his pet name. His real name is Nikolai Mihailovich Gorbachev, and he's the commander of an armored division in the Bakony Mountains."

"Well, I'm a painter, and I live in Óbuda."

"But I'm sure I called the right number."

"In that case, something's not right between us."

"What do you mean by not right?"

"I was referring to the telephone company."

"That's different."

* The original version of the one minute story entitled "Historical Mistake".

** "Do you speak Russian?" Like its final version, this short piece is a reference to the absurdity of the Russians "calling "on the Hungarians in 1944, then forgetting to leave. However, due to its pointed references, it could not be published until after the democratic change in government in 1989.

# headlines

Due to an unlawful pass from the right the Erkel choir of the Smalltraders' Cooperative are scheduled to sing in Romania quadruplets born in a station master's booth all healthy used tommy gun to make off with 7 million in cash from bank Mrs. J. Pucskó, 78, invited to attend tiger hunt by Duke of Kent died four times but is doing well as prize of pickles remains stable Carter's report on the tsunami in Cambodia just published why Hungarian soccer is declining too much sewage in the Tisza premier at the National Theater tomorrow with poor visibility, sleet, and slippery roads

# meat loaf

Combine the ground meat with a whole egg, a roll soaked in milk, season with a dash of salt and black pepper, shape into small loafs, and fry in hot lard or oil.

*Note:* For us mammals, it is not inconsequential whether we grind the meat, or we end up in the grinder ourselves.

*1968*

# the age of aggression

A court sentenced senior internist Dr. Tivadar Senye of the 7th district clinic to two years of corrective training for forcibly administering first aid to Mrs. Sebestyén Kovács of Budapest as she lay unconscious and profusely bleeding after a car ran her over in front of the clinic gate.

The same court sentenced Richárd Kozák, 87, to one year's probation for refusing to rape Amália B., a 34 year old newspaper vendor.

Neither of the defendants have appealed.

*1979*

# aiming for the salt cellar

The entire family, nuclear plus extended, plus Ursula, a very attractive sixteen-year-old from Warnemünde, were sitting around the dinner table. Ursula was an exchange child. She'd already been taken on a tour of Budapest and had been to Lake Balaton, so it was now time to introduce her to Hungarian cooking. The family went all out. They made her fish soup, chicken paprika with sour cream, and three kinds of strudel. They were still eating the chicken paprika when Károly Valkó looked around and said, "Where is the salt?"

Because of Ursula, everything had to be said in German as well. But Valkó wasn't just asking, he was also hoping for an answer, a smile for a smile. But in the hubbub, nobody paid the least attention to him.

*"Der Saltz?"* he asked, flashing a smile at Ursula.

*"Das Saltz,"* Ursula said, smiling back and pointing to the salt cellar before her attention turned to some other matter, alas.

The salt cellar was within easy reach, or so Valkó thought. Since he'd turned fifty, his left eye had been gradually weakening, and he was living in constant fear that his driver's license would not be renewed. Despite his glasses, he could never gauge distances properly.

He reached a hand for the salt cellar. No good. He reached even further, hoping that someone would help, but Tildi, his younger daughter, was busy passing the *galushka* around.

*"Das sind die ungarischen galushka."*

*"Nudeln?"* the pretty young thing from Warnemünde asked, because she was not familiar with anything except noodles.

*"Nich Nudeln, sondern galushka,"* Mrs. Valkó explained, and everybody laughed.

Meanwhile, ignored by all, the corpulent head of the family leaned over the table, veritably sprawling on top. He climbed up, and in his much worn black lace-up shoes found himself standing on the snow-white tablecloth. Still, nobody paid him the least attention; they were busy with Ursula, explaining to her the secret of making good dill pickles, which was not easy, because nobody knew the German word for dill. And so, ignored by all, Valkó started walking diagonally across the tabletop, aiming for the salt cellar.

"Two steps," he reasoned, "and I will have made it."

But that was wishful thinking. Needless to say, the salt cellar remained where it was; on the other hand, the whole table with everything on it and everyone around it seemed to have grown in size. The small objects became large, and the large objects became larger still. The small bowl that had been put out for the pickles was now as huge as the basin of a fountain, and a toothpick that was lying around looked more like a prefabricated concrete beam. (Valkó was the stock manager at Construction Company No. 71, hence the simile.) Little wonder if in this expanding universe Valkó walked on and on, faster and faster, but the salt cellar seemed no closer, even though it had not moved out of reach.

Because a voice inside was urging him on – "Go! Go! Go!" – it was too late to turn back. In his excitement Valkó didn't even realize that the diners around the table had fallen silent. He broke into a run, but then he recalled that due to a bad cardiac valve, his physician had advised him against climbing stairs, much less running. He stopped and, panting, took a look around.

He was in luck. He just had to step over the blade of a knife the size of a sword to be near his car, a Fiat 1500. The car was a gift from his brother-in-law, whom some shady business dealings had sent straight to Canada. He opened the door and plopped down behind the steering wheel.

The windows were frozen, and he had trouble starting up the engine. It took him several minutes to warm it up. But then, slowly and cautiously, he headed for the snowfield. (Ever since he'd gauged the distance badly once in the middle of Margaret Bridge and slid under the crane of a salvage truck, caution had become second nature to him, even though he'd been lucky, in a way, because he found his car hooked to the crane.)

Now in the snow, though, he was even more careful than usual. He drove around the bread crumbs that were lying disorderly all over the place and put his foot on the break whenever he encountered a crease in the tablecloth. However, his efforts were in vain. He'd hardly gone ten or twelve kilometers when he bashed head on into a traffic sign.

He knocked it over, and the cooler crushed the motor, which went dead. Valkó checked the sign sunk in the snow. It said *"To the salt cellar"*, which was quite unnecessarily, one might add, because the salt cellar was clearly visible, even though it, too, was sunk in the snow. His wife, on the other hand, was not as easy to spot, because she had merged into one with the white haze of the wintry snowfield. She was laughing. She must have said something wrong in German, Valkó thought as he continued trekking knee deep in snow.

The upper layer had turned to ice, making progress difficult, but he continued trekking because he'd reached the point of no return where not even the leaden weight of his lace-ups, to which clumps of snow had adhered, could dissuade him. His last bit of strength was about to desert him when his proverbial good luck came to his aid, and as if by magic, a dog sled came into view.

At first he smiled. Funny thing, he thought, bemused, a dog sled on the table, but then his good spirits left him and he turned grave and emotional as he remembered *Scott's Last Expedition*, the favorite book of his youth on which he conferred all the hero worship and romantic yearnings of his adolescent years. He merely had to close his eyes and presto, he became the English ship's captain who froze to death at the South Pole. And now – for such is life – there he stood, balding and with a bad heart, in that tragic six day snow storm, whipping the dozen or so strong, long haired South Pole dogs into a run.

His situation, perilous to begin with, was growing more and more perilous by the minute. The mercury in the thermometer had dropped, and he had neither a tent nor a piece of zwieback, not even a kerosene stove. His dogs, too, buckled under one by one, because he had no dog food to give them. But he continued relentlessly driving the sled for three days and three nights without food or drink, shivering with cold, advancing in the hope of a hopeless rescue, until on the night of the third day the last dog also collapsed on him.

Nothing but snowfields and silence as far as the eye could see. The horizon empty, his family and relatives gone, his wife, even the radiant beauty of the girl from Warnemünde, all gone. Only a tiny, golden tongue of flame flickered against the black sky next to the salt cellar, because his daughter Tildi had insisted that two candles be placed on the dinner table in honor of their German guest. The stock manager regarded the flickering flame with awe. "Good Lord," he heard himself say, "the Northern light!" Meanwhile, the ice was slowly creeping up his leg.

He took a small appointment book from his pocket in which he kept track of his business trips, and with his frozen fingers and a nearly frozen fountain pen, he wrote, *God save the King,* whereas he'd been a social democrat all his life, and certainly no royalist. Then something else emerged from his youth and he added, *Long live England,* whereas he'd never been to that verdant isle either. The one place he had his heart set on was Italy, but the previous year, when he finally got a passport, he didn't dare set out on such a long journey with just seventy dollars in his pocket.*

*1968*

* After travel was liberalized, and people could apply for passports once every three years, allowing them to take only $70 with them was an expedient way of keeping them at home.

# four theses

final deductions drawn from an exchange of views with a prominent philosopher of antiquity (Plato) that, by refuting everything we held to be true thus far, point the way to the foundation of a new, profound and wide-ranging view of the world and is guaranteed, besides, to rule out the possibility of error. (With the original Greek graphs.)

1

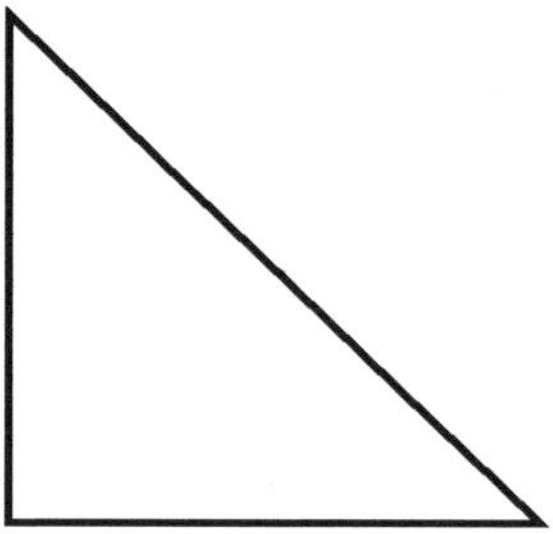

The graph seen above is not, as the popular notion would have it, a "right angled triangle". It is neither at a right angle, nor is it a triangle. Those who are incapable of understanding this are laboring under a false hypothesis and have no one to blame for the consequences but themselves.

2

The assertion that the graph seen above is a "length of measure" which, to add insult to injury, is identical to "one centimeter", is imprecise and not amenable to proof. All measurements based on this assertion, not to mention the entire decimal system, are therefore arbitrary and their use will gravely disappoint those who doggedly insist on it.

3

**f**

The assertion that the above graph represents the letter *f* is naive and without scientific foundation. Accordingly, all its adherents, no matter how illustrious (including the best writers and philosophers) are responsible not only for hindering the self-realization of the above sign or symbol, but are also fettering the free flight of their own fancy.

4

•

This dot is a dot.
Since it has no spatial dimension, the assertion made above cannot be refuted and may be considered as given. All deductions based on it – provided they do not violate the bounds of the above assertion – may be considered generally valid which, in retrospect, puts mankind's past in a new light and, not allowing for the possibility of error will even reveal – indeed, veritably force us to accept – a more sensible future.

*1978*

# homo sapiens

1

Everything we grasp with our conscious mind is merely an assertions.

2

Some of these assertions are false, while others are true.

3

With an eye to the above, we reject the false assertions and embrace the true assertions. In short, the way in which we judge our assertions bears within it the possibility of the search for truth.

4

Man is the only living creature endowed with the capacity of searching for the truth, because only he can reject or embrace a given possibility. Thus, truth is embodied in the image of the thinking man.

5

This capacity of ours has made it possible for us to triumph over the forces of nature, to cure the sick, to put an end to slavery, to love our neighbors as ourselves, and to plan the future with a view towards bringing about the best of all possible worlds.

6

In this manner, we have thus wiped hatred and sin, war and strife, sadness and penury off the face of the earth and are living in good cheer, security, and happiness.

7

Provided our sense of judgment will not be impaired, this state of well being should hold out for all time to come.

*1979*

# ballad
# about the magic of poetry

The telephone booth stood on Grand Boulevard. Its door opened and closed at regular intervals as people went about their daily business, tried to clear up their petty affairs, called the electric company, made dates for the night, asked friends for a quick loan, or tortured their loved ones with their jealousy. Once when an elderly lady hung up, she leaned against the phone and cried. But such occurrences were rare.

Then on a sunny summer afternoon, a poet entered the booth. He picked up the phone and called his editor. " I have the last four lines," he announced.

He next read the four lines of poetry from a soiled sheet of paper.

"That's depressing," his editor said, "rewrite it. And make sure it's cheerful this time."

The poet tried to reason with him, but in vain. He put the receiver back in its cradle and left the booth.

For a while no one came, and the phone booth stood empty. But then a woman approached. She was appreciably past her prime. She had an exceptionally heave frame and ample breasts, and she was clothed in a light cotton dress with large floral print. She tried to open the phone booth door.

The door opened only with difficulty. At first it wouldn't even give. But when it did, it flew open with such force, the woman was veritably propelled back onto the sidewalk. When she tried again, the door did something to her that could best be described as a kick. The woman reeled back and fell against a nearby mail box.

The people waiting at the bus stop crowded around her. A man with a briefcase – someone, clearly, to be reckoned with – tried to open the door, but it slammed into him with such force, he fell flat on his back on the hard pavement.

Meanwhile, quite a crowd had gathered around the booth, making comments on it, the post office, and the woman in the large floral print dress. Some people swore that the door was wired for high voltage, while others said the corpulent woman in the large floral print dress must have had an accomplice, and were trying to steal the coins from the booth, but were caught red handed.

For a while the phone booth listened to their confused accusations in silence, then it turned around and began walking down Rákóczi Road at its leisure. When it reached the corner the light had just turned red, so it stopped and waited.

The people watched it go, but nobody said anything. In this part of the world nothing causes a sensation unless it is natural. Meanwhile, the bus pulled up, the people disappeared into its belly, and the phone booth continued its leisurely stroll down Rákóczi Road.

It was in the best of spirits. It did some window shopping, then it stopped in front of a florist. Some people thought they'd seen it enter a book shop, but they may have mistaken it for someone else. Anyway, it stopped by a small pub on a side street for a shot of brandy, then walked along the Danube and crossed over to Margaret Island. On the Island it spotted another phone booth by the ruins of a convent. It went passed it, then turned around, and having made up its mind about something, crossed the road and discretely but unflinchingly began giving the other booth the eye. Later, as the sun was going down, it headed for the rose bushes, trampling some of the roses under foot.

We have no way of knowing what may or may not have occurred by the ruins that night, because the public lighting on the Island is not up to par, to say the least. Be that as it may, the next morning early risers were surprised to see that the booth in front of the ruined convent was packed with crimson roses, and throughout the day, it kept giving the wrong number. The other phone booth had disappeared without a trace.

At the break of dawn it left the Island and crossed over to Buda. It climbed to the top of Gellért Hill, then made its way, through hill and dale, to the peak of Hármashatár Hill. Then it descended the slope and headed for the highway, whereafter it was never seen in Budapest again.

Outside the city limits, past the very last houses of Hűvösvölgy but on this side of Nagykovácsi, lies a meadow of wild flowers, just big enough for a small child to skip around it without running out of breath. Because of the tall trees, it is as well hidden from sight as a mountain lake. It is too small, even, for anyone to bother taking a scythe to it, and so by midsummer the grass, weeds and flowers come up waist high. This is the spot where the phone booth camped down.

People who pass by it on their Sunday outings are delighted to see it. It makes them feel like playing a practical joke on someone who is still fast asleep, or they remember to call home and ask that the keys they'd left behind be placed under the mat. They enter the booth, which stands awry, sunk into the soft ground, and as the long stemmed flowers of the field lean in after them, they take the receiver off the hook.

The phone, however, will not connect them. Instead, they hear four lines of a poem coming from the headpiece as softly as the strains of a muted violin. The phone does not return their deposited coins either. But no one has ever complained.

*1961*

## when it comes to the most complicated matters we often understand each other perfectly well but when it comes to simple things more often than not we don't

"How do you do. Is this where I can rent an inflatable rubber mat?"

"What was that?"

"Is this the place where I can rent an inflatable rubber mat? I was told that this green shed is the beach depot of the Home Trade Ministry, and you rent inflatable rubber mats."

"This is the beach depot of the Home Trade Ministry. But we rent only beach chairs, water skis, and inflatable rubber mats."

"That's great. We'd like two inflatable rubber mats, please."

"I don't understand. *Sprechen Sie deutsch*?"

*"Nicht deutsch."*

"I speak some French. *Vooz sprechen fransay*?"

*"Nicht fransay."*

"Well then, what language do you speak?"

"I only speak Hungarian."

"Very funny. Why don't you speak Hungarian then?"

"I am speaking Hungarian. I'm Hungarian. I was born Hungarian. Hungarian is the only language I speak. What's the rental on inflatable rubber mats?"

"Don't try that trick on me. I'm a third year history and philosophy major. I'm down here for the summer to make some pocket money."

"Good for you."

"I work half a day and spend the other half on the beach.

And for your information, that's my boyfriend over there, and he's on the national pentathlon team."

"Why are you so sarcastic?"

"Because I rent only beach chairs, water skis, and inflatable rubber mats. If you have any funny business in mind, you're barking up the wrong tree."

"I have no funny business in mind, believe me. I just want to rent two inflatable rubber mats."

*"Bei uns ist vollkommene Glaubensfreiheit."*

"What did you say?"

"I said there's freedom of religion here. Tourists usually ask us if they can attend mass on Sunday."

"Look here. You studied logic. Let's try to talk logically."

"What an interesting language you speak! Logic. It's the same in Hungarian."

"Since you've brought up freedom of religion, let me ask you. Do you believe in God?"

"Only like Kierkegaard, in his realization, if you know what I mean."

"More or less. That someone floating above a depth of 70,000 knots should still be happy... Are you familiar with Teilhard de Chardin?"

"He was not compulsory, but I read two of his works in German."

"What do you think of him?"

"I was awed at first, thinking he was *the* modern genius... But when it came to the decisive question, when he tries to reconcile science and religion, he reaches a dead end."

"I couldn't agree with you more. But if we see eye to eye so well, why can't we get from A to B over two silly rubber mats?"

"Voulez voo to rent kelkeshoses?"

"Here we go again. And yet we can both think sensibly.

You know what? Let's narrow the topic. What would you say if I were to ask for two beach chairs?"

"No problem. With or without umbrellas?"

"Very good. And now, tell me. Have you got water skis?"

"They come in three sizes. Which one would you like?"

"I wouldn't. I want two inflatable rubber mats."

"Two what?"

"Interesting. We can't seem to come to head over this one thing."

"What thing?"

"The rubber mat. It's a compound word. Rubber, plus mat. You do know rubber? Like rubber soles? Rubber tires?"

"Of course."

"What about mats?"

"You think I'm stupid or something?"

"Okay. Let's combine the two. Give me two rubber mats."

"You don't seem to understand. We rent only beach chairs, water skis, and inflatable rubber mats."

"In that case, I apologize."

"Don't mention it."

"Good bye."

"And good bye to you, too."

*1967*

# embarrass de richesses

“Good morning, mam.”

“What can I do for you, sir?”

“I’d like to purchase a brown hat.”

“Any particular type? Something sporty? Traditional? Wide-brimmed?”

“Which would you recommend?”

“How about this one? It’s quite versatile. Not too dark, not too light. Take a look in the mirror.”

“It suits me very well.”

“It’s got your name written all over it.”

“All the same, could you show me another style, please?”

“Of course. This one will look just as smashing.”

“And so it does. I wish I knew which one to buy.”

“Why don’t you try a third? We get a lot of complements on this model, and it will look just as becoming on you as the first two.”

“Indeed. And how much does it cost?”

“They all cost the same.”

“What about the quality?”

“The quality, too, is identical, I can assure you.”

“In that case, what is the difference between the three hats I just tried on?”

“There’s no difference at all. I haven’t even got three brown men’s hats.”

“How many have you got?”

"Just this one."
"The one I tried on three times in a row?"
"Yes, sir. So which one will you take?"
"I can't quite make up my mind. Maybe the first."
"It looked very smart on you. Not that the other two didn't."
"Still, I think I'll stick with the first one."
"An excellent choice, sir. Enjoy it."

*1975*

# hungaricum

A new animals species has just been registered at the Zoological Conference at The Hague. Bred at the Borsod-based research facility of the Hungarian Animal Breeding Institute, the new species has been registered under the name of Improlific Scraper (Varians Hungaricus).

The Improlific Scraper can not only scrape but, with proper training and adequate practice, it can even cover up the small holes it digs up. It can furthermore catch mice and rats, act as a watch dog, translate French drawing room comedy, manufacture precision instruments, put out forest fires, do certified public accounting, teach philosophy, and even fill in for a head of state. Its judgments are level headed, its decisions well-founded; its actions are invariably goal oriented, and its critical faculties are irreproachable. Considering its usefulness, its consumption – it uses up just 2,500 to 3,000 calories per day – is inconsequential.

The scientists at Borsod call it improlific because they have succeeded in breeding just one specimen which, for lack of a mate, cannot reproduce.

*1975*

# has anyone seen...?

At 5:30 p.m. on the 7th of this month, Mrs. K. Fehér, née Márta Flügl, headed for the movies and hasn't been seen since. Mrs. Fehér, 41, a resident of Budapest, has been alternately described as tall or short, prone to gain weight or lean and lanky. Her eyes are blue or green, possibly black. Her hair color can not be determined. Her winter coat is dark blue or rust brown, though possibly gray, with fur trimming. (Correction: the trim is not fur but velvet, though the coat may have no trimming at all.) Special distinctive marks: female.

Any leads will be greatly appreciated by:

*her worried husband*

# empty page*

* These "empty pages" are about nonexistent things or else things that exist, but about which the author has nothing to say.

# inventory

hilly landscape (after storm)
3 cumulus clouds
1 fish pond
1 cabin for man overseeing the levy
1 man (leaning out the window)
1 shout
1 line of poplars
1 muddy footpath
bicycle tracks (in the mud)
1 women's bicycle
1 shout (louder than the previous one)
1 pair of sandals
1 skirt (flapping in the wind, beating against the luggage wrack)
1 flower print blouse
1 amalgam filling (in a tooth)
1 woman (young)
1 shout (louder than the previous two)
new bicycle tracks
1 window closing
silence

*1968*

# so much to keep in mind

Valid for travel within two prepaid zones within one hour of initial embarkation with a maximum of four transfers on the shortest possible route between your starting point and final destination. Transfer is permitted only at crossings, junctions and line terminals, and is restricted to cars, trains, buses and trolleys whose route must not be identical to the routes already taken. Only one Danube bridge may be crossed en route, and each station may be touched only once. *Attention:* No detours or breaks allowed.

*1963*

# except for you

József Gerván, a railway worker, died at the shunting yard in Rákoskeresztúr when a wagon backed up and ran over him. He was thirty three

Mrs. Vilmos Sugár, née Lenke Dvornik, everyone's favorite Lenci Mama, after a protracted illness she bore with pious forbearance

little Évi Poch, aged seven

Sándor Baltazár, our company's trusted employee of long standing, in the line of duty, in London, tragically, in the prime of life

in the 9th district, in front of Üllői út 84, tram number 42, Mrs. Bálint Boros, a widow, who stepped in front of the car within breaking distance

Mihály Rózsa, a plumber, at sixty one

the plane's passengers Árpád Fodor, Mrs. Árpád Fodor, Anikó Fodor, Imre Nardai and three other as yet unidentified victims

Albert Hollós

Rozália Kerkó

and many others

except for you

# I buy my book

When a book comes out, the author is entitled to thirty complementary copies, a mere pittance, really.* As soon as he receives them, he sets about dedicating them. Wife, Mom, Dad, Uncle Ede, Aunt Eta, a couple of distant relatives, easily offended, writer friends, dentist, present girlfriend, one or two, sometimes three, former girlfriends. Though it is not of the essence here, it might be worth pointing out the intricate web of dedicatory relationships that exist between writers – who can be sent a copy through the mail, who needs to be given a copy personally, who merits "with love", "with sincere friendship", "friendship", or just his name in lieu of a dedication. It is all part of an intricate ritual. I won't attempt to explain these intricacies, because I don't think I could do it; I have just enough wits about me to avoid major disaster.

The point is that once a writer has depleted the stack of the thirty complementary copies, he's left with nothing for himself and suffers an anxiety attack thinking he's bound to have forgotten a number of people who are even now flinging stones at the window pane of his consciousness.

The last time, too, I neglected a number of important people, so while walking down Grand Boulevard, I stalked into a bookshop intending to buy six extra copies.

Under the circumstances, an author can say, how do you do, I'm so and so, and I'm looking for a book I wrote entitled

* Note: The story was written in 1952.

such and such. Or he can say, I'd like the book entitled such and such, written by so and so. The choice he makes invariably reveals something about his character. But regardless of what it might reveal about me, I always go with the second option. Of course, the situation is awkward either way. But at least it's not written all over me that I feel how awkward the situation is.

However, back to the bookshop. The saleslady, who has wiry black hair and oily skin, is around forty years of age. The fact that she loves books is written all over her, and when she takes the volume I've requested off the shelf, she wipes the jacket clean with the sleeve of her uniform.

"A lovely book," she says, handing it to me.

"Do you really think so?" I ask. "Have you read it?"

"Yes."

"Is it really that good?" I urge, because it's better to hear such things twice than once.

"Yes," she says with conviction.

I open the book, leafing through it at random. "In that case," I say, "I'll take five more."

"Five?" the saleslady asks, her eyes ferreting me out.

"Five," I say, feeling very foolish.

"In short, six copies in all?" she asks with an edge to her voice.

"Provided you have that many," I say apologetically.

"I do," she says, forgetting to veil the censure in her voice.

She slowly reaches up to the shelf where two more volumes are leaning against their neighbors. She wipes the dust jackets clean with the back of her sleeve, then places them in front of me. She looks hopeful. She's probably hoping I'll be satisfied with three copies.

But how could I be satisfied with three copies when I need six? I pick up each book in turn, study the title page, and after ascertaining that each contains the same exact words, I stack them up. I wait.

"Am I to understand you want three more?"

"Yes, please."

"Is it for a school?" she asks, trying to make sense of my request.

"No," I say. "It's for private use."

"I see," she says.

She sounds upset, unsure of herself. Her behavior undergoes a dramatic change. She takes a ladder, climbs to the top, and comes down with an armful of books. But this time she does not wipe them clean. As she writes out my bill, she keeps glancing up at me, trying to make me out from behind her glasses. I can tell that by now she's even taken objection to my nose. I must be up to no good, except she can't figure out what it might be, because a book is a special, unique something, quite unsuited to hoarding, and so it's not suited for speculation on the market either.* One book is as good as a hundred. You can read a book as often as you like, and you can lend it to others to read. You can do all sorts of thing with a book. The one thing you can not do with a book is buy two or more copies of it. It doesn't make sense. What, the saleslady wondered, could my racket be?

"Are you a librarian?" she asks hopefully.

"No, of course not," I say, turning as red as a beet.

I take the receipt. I go to the cashier and pay. On the way back I remember Dr. U., who had been over the night before to visit our child but wouldn't take any money. Unfortunately, I will need a seventh copy as well.

I dare not look the saleslady in the eye, so I give her a sideways glance. I see the agitated lines of her face, the hair falling

* In 1952, when there was a shortage of just about everything, people could go to jail for keeping ("hoarding") too much sugar or flour at home, activities punishable by law.

limp over her forehead, the glasses on the bridge of her nose leaning to one side like a hussar who has received a deadly blow.

"Will there be anything else?" she asks, her voice trembling.

"No, thank you," I say.

I stuff the books in my briefcase and leave.

There's a bookshop on Grand Boulevard just across the way, but I give it a wide berth and start off in the opposite direction because, glancing over my shoulder, I see the window pane of the shop, and behind it, a pair of darkly gleaming bespectacled eyes pinned for all they're worth on my back. I do my darnest to merge with in the crowd.

*1952*

# the death of the viewer

Having announced themselves well in advance, eight or ten actors (which is how many are generally needed for a play) show up at the viewer's house at the appointed time. Some have come by bus, others by cab, still others by car (the few who own one), all of them at exactly 7 p.m., which is curtain time, except for Sunday matinées.

They leave their outer garments in the hall, enter, take their seats and sit quietly or converse in a light whisper. Though he does not show it, the viewer has butterflies in his stomach. Nevertheless, he tries to act natural, as if his guests weren't even there. After all, the show has already begun.

He stands up, sits down, ruminates, pours water into a kettle, and makes tea. But he only pretends to be drinking the tea because his thoughts are elsewhere, and everyone can feel it, even though his face is a blank, he blows his nose, and yawns. But then he suddenly throws all restraint to the wind. He takes a step forward. His voice trembles, and he makes a confession of love. Though the object of his love is far away, he, while delivering the monologue, acts as if she were there with him, encouraging him with a smile.

Many other things happen besides. For instance, the phone rings, and we can tell that the news the viewer has received have not been good. His youthful movements become leaden, the light in his eyes dims, and soon after, his hair turns gray. Next, he clutches his side, where the pain is at its worst – clearly gall bladder or kidney stones.

He undergoes a dramatic change. He has stopped pretending. His face is sunken, he has lost interest in all people and things, his father, his younger sister, even his wife. The pain proves persistent, and it becomes increasingly clear that he will not make it.

He would give anything to hide from the prying eyes of the actors, if only he could; after all, even a brute beast likes to die in the privacy of his own lair. But like it or not, he, the viewer, is destined to die on the scene, which takes quite some time, longer than one would expect, because death is a struggle, except, who would have thought that it would be such a long one!

Poor viewer, he hasn't got much left, but he gathers up his remaining strength again and again. He remembers one thing or another that he tells the actors about, nothing of real consequence and nothing particularly enlightening, but issuing, as they do, from the lips of a dying man, they sound touching all the same.

Thrashing about on the floor, gasping for breath, with a rattle in his throat, he gives up the ghost. The actors clap their hands together as they start gathering their belongings, and once out on the street, they discuss the viewer's actions, whether they were authentic enough, especially his death throes, and if they are satisfied, they go back to the theater and share the viewer's address with the other actors, adding that they can look forward to an intriguing and entertaining night.

*1969*

## what is art?

Just about every Molière play ends with an official and his scribe being summoned and either a marriage contract or a last will and testament being drawn up. It was due to this circumstance that F. O. could take up his final position on stage during the first rehearsal. The main characters had to pretend to be skirting around furniture that was indicated only by chalk marks on the floor, while he already had his scribe's lectern, which had done duty in several earlier Molière plays. Though the small stand was partly hidden from view by the baldachin of the sick bed, it was fully equipped with paper, ink well, and in the ink well, two feather quills.

"You won't be up to your old tricks again, Feri, will you," the director asked turning to him.

"What an idea," O. shot back, "I wouldn't dream of it."

He'd been in the theatre for twenty-six years. The previous year, which was his jubilee, he received a diploma, a bottle of champagne, and some congratulatory words. Still, during the quarter of a century he'd been with the theater, the most he could hope for was a chance to deliver a sentence or two, a welcome departure from his usual silent parts. He kept trying to make something out of nothing, but the consequences were disastrous, so this time he was determined to heed the director's warning.

He sat down by the small lectern and without a peep, practically as if he weren't there at all, he took down the last will and testament of the dying father. By the sixth rehearsal, however, he began sneezing, hawking, and clearing his throat. He put down the quill, took out an oversize handkerchief printed with bright red squares, and blew his nose so loud you'd think it was a trumpet. That much human interest, he felt, he could afford to sneak in.

However, the third time around, the director caught on.

"Got a cold, Feri old boy?" he asked.

"Seems so," Feri said. "I wonder where I picked it up."

He couldn't sleep for two nights. He blamed himself. He was sorry he'd resorted to something as trivial as blowing his nose. He wondered how he could enhance the figure of the scribe from inside. Then he had a brain storm.

Three days later he inched his lectern forward just a bit. It seemed like a safe move. After all, half his face was still hidden behind the brocade draperies, so who could take exception? But from behind the draperies he shot piercing, then disparaging, then disdainful glances at the dying father. Why? Because, as a result of the sleepless nights, the scribe had grown to manhood in the countryside as a fatherless outcast, with never a kind word from anyone. He had always envied those who had a father, and now, as he officiated by the dying man's bedside, his soul was in turmoil. It was the first time he'd come face to face with a father who was disinheriting his son in his will.

He was too distraught to write. He kept glancing up, his eyes full of derision.

The actor playing the dying father was quite unnerved.

"Why are you staring at me like that?" he asked.

The director came over.

"Up to your old trick again, Feri old boy?"

"I'm just reacting," he said in great pain, "because he's such a bad father."

"Well," the director shouted, "don't react, write!"

He heaved a great sigh, dipped the quill into the ink well

and resumed writing. For several days afterwards, he couldn't come up with anything. Then something began to take shape, and in the end, there it was!

At first, nothing happened. His countenance like a piece of stone, he sat by the lectern and took down what was dictated to him. But then he puckered his lips. It wasn't his fault if the old quill pen got clogged up. He shook it out. He put it in his mouth and licked it clean. But even so, it made an ink blot on the paper! Annoyed, he shook his head. He tried the other quill, but fared no better. The few insiders who were sitting in on the rehearsal were riveted to his struggle with the quills. They couldn't take their eyes off of him. He then took out a penknife and began sharpening one of the quills. He was just about to try it out when the father, who gave out his last death rattle, raised himself on his elbow.

The rehearsal was cut short. There was an exchange of sharp, harsh, and indelicate words. But let's not dwell on these humiliating details.

F .O. became despondent, and for days afterward, he wrote in silence like an automaton. But the premier broke him. Just moments before curtain time – he was still in his dressing room – he came up with a brand new approach to his character, one that, despite its daring, no one could possibly fault.

He asked for a piece of black gauze. They gave him linen. No matter, it would have to do.

When the curtain went up, the scribe entered the scene with a mourning band on his arm. Since he was dressed in black anyway, nobody noticed the narrow band. His face was calm, even serene. No one could have possibly known that he had just lost his only daughter, the consolation of his old age, his beloved Jennie. He sat down and began to write. His soul was in turmoil, for the sight of the dying father brought back memories of his own dead Jennie. When the father breathed his last, it was all he could do to suppress a tear, but with superhuman effort he suppressed it and, indeed, no one was ever the wiser.

The show was a resounding success. The critics heaped praise upon praise on the actors. But they had eyes only for the showy, superficial characterizations. No one mentioned the scribe, even in passing. O. shrugged it off. What do they know about art! One must produce something extraordinary even if no one is looking. But was it worth it, he wondered. Yes, it most certainly and indubitably was.

*1966*

# no sooner is one dilemma solved than another rears its ugly head

A small mignonette went to the washroom and sat on the toilet. Then it remembered that it was just a plant, it had neither bowels, nor bowel movement. So what was it doing on the toilet?

Well, that got cleared up, at least! The small mignonette straightened up and without having accomplished what it had come for, rejoined the guests. When the hostess (who had the blood of English royalty trickling in her veins and whose name day was being celebrated just then) threw a quizzical glance its way it smiled back, but all it could say by way of explanation was, "There has been a slight misunderstanding."

Then it headed for the cocktail bar, because it felt like having a glass of champagne. "Wouldn't it be a riot," it thought when it caught sight of the lovely long stemmed glasses, "if it were to turn out that I can't drink either!"

*1969*

## for a keepsake album

"Who are you, you lovely, long haired, slender young maiden?"

"My full name is Klára Nóra Annamária Olga Vorazlicki. But they call me Noodle. And who are you, old man?"

"My name is also Klára Nóra Annamária Olga Vorazlicki, and they also call me Noodle."

"How curious. You're old, bald, and your right eye is stuck all the way up in its socket. I don't think I understand."

"You must learn, Noodle, that there are no two identical Klára Nóra Annamária Olga Vorazlickis in the world."

"What a shame!"

"And so it is."

*1972*

# a grain of rice laments

I'm sorry for taking up your precious time, but I'm worried about the future, and I need someone to talk to. My habitual debating partner, my friend and neighbor thrice removed (meaning that there are two grains of rice between us), has a kind heart and a good head, but is far too adamant about his rather extreme views.

The object of our dispute is easy enough. It can be put very simply. Are we grains of rice identical? What does the future hold in store for us? And what will our descendants be like?

The sad fact of the case is that we are a superior species, the so-called "winter-resistant Tibetan" strain. Not only do we take the cold better than most other rice, we're superior in other respects as well, our starch content and reproductive capacity, to name just two. What the future holds for the other strains I'd rather not even consider. We have enough problems of our own. After being planted, we sprout, head up, and bring seed, and this is boring, even I will admit. My friend has a more pointed way of putting it. "We're just repeating ourselves," he says, at which point I bring up Mendel, saying that with time, we will evolve and bring forth new strains. But he just shrugs and quotes Li Tai-ling's maxim, "Only renewal leads to eternity. He that cannot differ is as good as dead."

This is the point where I generally lose my patience. Once I held a mirror up to him. "Is this what you call identical? Well? Is it?" But he just turned sarcastic on me. He was still smiling when – lucky that he is – the mailman came, a has-been intellectual wearing a pair of glasses.

He called to me from a distance.

"Rice! You got mail!"

He calls me rice. We rice don't have names. Why should we? Two types of cheese, two brands of toothpaste, two novels, they need names to set them apart. But two grains of rice? We don't even address our envelopes. Anyway, I opened the envelope, took a quick look at its contents, then gave it back.

"I know I'm just a grain of rice," I said, hurt to the quick, "still, I don't appreciate being mistaken for somebody else."

Over the course of his life, a grain of rice comes into contact with two to three hundred thousand other grains of rice on the average. I know, because our brain capacity allows us to remember that many. With us rice, not recognizing someone is considered a serious offense, especially when it comes to mailmen, who should know better. So you can imagine the mailman's embarrassment.

Needless to say, he tried to make light of the matter. "Oh, how silly of me," he stammered, "I'm so absent minded these days. Must be the weather."

Meanwhile he sneaked a look around as he spoke, the whites of his eyes flashing first at my neighbor to the right, then my first neighbor to my left, then the one after that, until his gaze came to rest on my friend.

"Oh, of course! It's for you! My lenses need cleaning."

"Not so fast!" my friend snorted. "If it's for me, why did you give it to him? Or is one rice like another to you?"

God, you should have seen that mailman! My friend flashed another sarcastic smile at me, and I thought I'd explode. I wish you could see us! Believe me, we're not at all alike. My friend is a Marxist (though he embraces only the idea of revolutionary aggression), while I started out as a Trotskyite, eventually siding with Gandhi, because I shy away from action of all kinds. That's splitting hairs, you say? Okay, okay. But just listen to a description of us separately.

He: Square shoulders, penetrating eyes, happy-go-lucky disposition. An insatiable appetite for pleasure, but he also likes to give. He'll take the shirt off his back for a kind word. He's an excellent swimmer and has trophies for saving a number of lives.

Me: Soft and round, gentle, slightly effeminate. I like singing sweet chansons in my pleasant little voice, and when the mood is on me, I like to stand under the blue moon, knee-deep in water, entertaining a whole field of rice. Special characteristics: when thrown in water, I sink like the Titanic.

It takes a mailman like him not to see the difference.

"So then, friend," I said turning to him, "there's no difference between us?"

He wrings his hands in embarrassment, his gaze skirts around, his brain working overtime.

"The difference is horrendous, if you please... *You* contain nearly eighty per cent starch!"

"What about him?"

Though come to think of it, what's the use of all this questioning? Might this insistence on being different from all others come from conceit and arrogance? After all, from the cradle through college, we were brought up in exactly the same way and receive the identical information from our environment which, in turn, is also loaded with identical information. If things go on like this, our grandchildren, too, will be exactly alike.

Still, I can't desist. I egg the mailman on until he gives in to pressure and concedes that we contain the same amount of starch. "It's even on the bag: Winter resistant Tibet rice. Starch content 80%."

Typical. Around these parts a mailman would rather die

than admit to having mixed up two individuals. I decide to pose an easier question.

"Listen," I say. "There's this river. You fell in. The current is sweeping you along and you're drowning. You're about to go under… And the two of us are standing on the shore, my friend and I. Got it? Well," I ask, "who jumps in the water? Him or me?"

His hand trembles. He points a shaking finger at me, then at my friend, then at me once again.

"Him," he says, his voice failing. "And you," he adds, pointing at me. "Neither of you would let me drown."

He actually said that, he really did, while – as you may know – the Valiant Lifeguard medal is pinned to my friend's lapel! It's sad. I don't know if others feel the same way, but when I see such a dim witted man with such faulty character suffer, I pity him, I really do. (Why not the brave and noble minded? But that's another story.)

"You know what," I say to him, "I won't ask any more questions. Go decide for yourself if there's anything to differentiate us, and don't feel obliged to answer. All the same, you might as well know that I have friends in high places at the post office."

And what do you think? Yes, that's right. That did the trick. I should have started with that right off.

"There is," he says instantly.

"Namely?"

"I need a piece of soap first."

"And then?"

"And also a piece of straw that has to be dipped in soap water."

"And then?"

"Then I have to blow into the piece of straw to make a bubble appear."

"And then?"

"Then the difference will become visible."

"In what way?"

"In... in...," he begins, the sweat running down his face, "the fact that his bubble will burst before yours."

Before mine? Did you hear that? I look triumphantly at my friend. He had it coming! For years he's been suffering from our assumed sameness, complaining right and left, whereas – and you are my witness – there are no two identical grain of rice anywhere in the world.

*1969*

# the final question

There was a horrendous bang on my door, then it split in two and came crashing down. There was a stranger standing on the threshold.

"Rascal, you are about to die!" he screamed at me.

I was just about to put kindling on the stove but hearing this, I straightened up.

"You must have mistaken me for someone else," I said.

"There's no mistake," he yelled again, though he'd forgotten to add rascal. "Your time is up!"

He reached for his back pocket to withdraw his gun, but he did it so slowly, with so much time to spare, you'd think he was stroking the back of a dog. In the meantime I stuffed the kindling in the stove and started a fire, then paced up and down my room, because before he's shot, a man likes to take account of his life. At this point the stranger's hand was still only half-way to his pocket; and what came next also happened with such languor you'd think you were watching a film in slow-motion.

Before I proceed, though, I'd like to make something clear. I know what people are like, and so I know that they will place what happened in the worst possible light. Accordingly, I would like to make it quite clear that the shooting took place with the usual expediency. The assassin was not slow; it was my assessment of the situation that was fast. (Fifteen times faster than the national average.) A man quick on the uptake sees more; he will even see things that would just be an indistinct blur in another person's eye. For instance, while someone yawns, I – provided I'm in top form – will consume a three-course meal. My assassin will probably swear that he finished me off in half a minute; but thanks to my quick wit, I was able to attend to various urgent matters.

Right now we're only at the point where the assassin has finally managed to produce his gun. There's no need to rush, but I'd like to make good use of the time at my disposal. What should I do? Hurl myself on the floor? Call for help? Fling something at the assassin's head? When a shooting drags on like this, it offers the victim no end of possibilities.

While he was finicking with his gun, I dialed my physician, who started complaining that the bevel wheel of his car was broken (the bevel wheel is part of the differential gear) and he had a hell of a time finding a new one. Only then did I get to put in a word edgewise.

"I haven't got much time, Doc. I'm about to be shot. Any suggestions?"

"That depends. Do you want to die or not?"

"I think I'd rather not."

"In that case, dodge the bullet," the perspicarious physician advised.

"If only it were that simple," I said. "A month from now I might suffer a stroke and end up a vegetable. The question is, should I really turn my back on a quick and easy death? Before I can make up my mind, I need to know the state of my health."

The doctor was very understanding. He itemized my sundry organic ills, then after giving it some thought, he said, "As one human being to another, I advise you to live. But as your doctor, I urge you not to pass up such a good opportunity."

"Thank you very much."

"Don't mention it."

While I was on the phone, my assassin pointed his gun at me, then slowly, very slowly, pulled the trigger. The bullet dragged itself across the room as sleepily as a fly in autumn. I waited, then dodged.

"How many bullets left?" I asked.

"Stop jumping around," my assassin said, "because there are only three bullets in the barrel."

"In short, there are two left," I said. "That leaves me plenty of time."

"You're a pain in the ass," my assassin said, chagrinned.

I quickly made a couple of phone calls. I took my leave of my loved ones and acquaintances, then called a writer friend who was thinking of buying a piece of real estate with his hard earned savings. I described the situation to him. From where I stand, I explained, value does not seem stable. Besides, the price of land is sure to go down. He thanked me for the good advice and for thinking of him, even at a time like this. I took my leave of him, too. That's when the second bullet reached me.

I gave it a whack with Simone de Beauvoir's *Mandarins*. The bullet hit the floor with a thud, then rolled under the bookcase. I looked around. A pile of unanswered letters lay on my desk. I sprang into action.

My letters were brief, but courteous. I backed out of exchanging my apartment for one in the 12th district, and gave advice to a young lady who was in love with two men at the same time. I called off a dinner engagement, a reader-writer event, and an invitation to be a godfather. It went without a hitch. But just as I was running out of time because the third bullet was heading in my direction, I found the last of the letters, which I'd been putting off answering for months, in which the League for Animal Rights from the local slaughterhouse had turned to me for advice.

"Please excuse us for inconveniencing you with our measly

problems, knowing how busy you are," it began, "but here at the slaughterhouse, we live ankle deep in blood, with the death-rattle of dying animals assaulting our ears, whereas we would like to remain true to the noble principle of the protection of animals. What do you advise?"

I don't have time to answer because the bullet, like a bluebottle, is just an arm's length away. And yet the question they've posed is not measly in the least, as they put it; it bears with universal significance, and may possibly be the most important question in the world.

A pity that even now, during the last possible moment, I haven't got a definitive answer. Still, I will see what I can do. Thanks to my quick wits, I still have a couple of seconds left. I might even come up with as many as ten solutions.

Or five.

Or three.

Or two.

Or one.

Sorry. Too late. You will have to go ask somebody else.

*1968*

# prose poems

## BALLAD ABOUT THE FIRST WORLD WAR

The following story was told by the Russian pilot Alexander Alexandrovich Falz-Fein, whom we'd taken as a prisoner, at the dinner we arranged in his honor.

"The Russian pilot, if he spots an enemy plane, can't get the better of his sportsmanship, and first sees the pilot in him, and only then the enemy. For instance, our pilots had great regard for the Hungarian-Austrian lieutenant Count M., whom they knew from personal experience to be a first rate pilot in the air and a chivalrous adversary, and were most fervent to please him in every way. Once in Galicia they captured a German lieutenant and a Hungarian captain, and the Russian pilots offered to take their letters to Count M. They proceeded to write the letters and the Russian pilots threw them down behind the Austrian-Hungarian lines in the usual white tin tube. At Easter, the Russian pilots threw down some cake addressed to Count M., and by way of a joke, added, 'Attention! Explosives!' In order to reciprocate this gesture of attentiveness, the following day Count M. had cigarettes thrown down behind the Russian lines addressed to those who had sent him the cake. Next they threw a letter down for Count M, in which they invited him for coffee the following day. Resorting to the same means of transport, Count M. countered that he'd rather not accept the sort of hospitality that might end in his imprisonment, which put an effective end to the exchange of letters; but a Russian pilot, unless he has no alternative, will not shoot at an enemy plane, because he feels a sense of solidarity. After all, they have an adversary in common, the air."

*(Ferenc Molnár, Memoirs of a War Correspondent, 1916)*

## BALLAD ABOUT HOME SICKNESS

Honored Comrade Stalin!

We, the undersigned, being POWs at Camp #241/b, are turning to you in order to request that you kindly give your stamp of approval to our setting up a Hungarian Legion.

The illustrious Red Army has already liberated part of our country, the Soviet tanks are entering our villages, the fighting continues on the streets of our towns and cities. We know that Comrade Stalin has already agreed to the setting up of a Czechoslovakian armored brigade, which has already been deployed. Arms in hand, the Hungarian banner flying overhead, we too would like to take out our share of crushing the fascist beast underfoot and liberating our country.

We read in the daily *True Word* that in other camps our fellow prisoners of war have also requested the setting up of a Hungarian Legion. We have further been informed that our senior officers Lieutenant General Stomm and Brigadier General Deseő have refused to command the Legion. However, we do not wish to identify ourselves with our senior officers and will willingly fight under the command of other officers, because Hungarians do not like to waste time, that's the way they are. We are on the side of the tens of thousands who want nothing as fervently as to fight for their homeland. We ask you, honored Comrade Stalin, to help us reach our goal.

Long live the Legion! Long live a liberated Hungary!

István János,
private first class

Zsigmond Nyitrai,
artillery corporal

András Hollós,
sergeant

Lajos Huszár,
enlisted man

and 354 others.

*(True Word, 1944)*

## BALLAD ABOUT THE BOMBING OF BUDAPEST

"Just imagine. I put my suitcase in Left Luggage at the station, and when I went back to get it, the suitcase was gone."

"That's nothing. I also put my suitcase in Left Luggage at the station, and by the time I went back to get it, the station was gone."

*(Contemporary joke, 1944)*

## BALLAD ABOUT EMIGRATION

I stand in front of King András's tomb in the wall of the Duomo feeling much relieved. This dead man is the only Hungarian in Naples that I know.

*(Sándor Márai, Diary, 1948)*

## BALLAD ABOUT SLEEPLESS NIGHTS

"Besides, we were often tolerant when faced with Rajk* and his gang's 'anti-Party attitude' and 'mistakes'. We did not suspect the hand of the enemy in these things, but the inexperience, want of practice and lack of education of the individuals in question. We were too lenient with them because not suspecting that we were dealing with traitors, we wanted to educate them and give them a chance to mend their ways.

"Also, until the Rajk case we had no similar affairs and the Comrades can imagine how shocked we were at the monstrous size of the treachery and baseness. We lacked practice in bringing such cases to light and knew that we could not go about it irresponsibly. It was not easy to come up with a plan for bringing the case to light, and I admit, it cost me many sleepless nights until the plan of action could take shape."

*(Mátyás Rákosi, Selected Articles and Speeches, 1949)*

## BALLAD ABOUT THE TRUTH

*Presiding Judge:* How did you meet with Mrazovich? Under what circumstances did he ask you to organize a hunt at your estate at Biritó-puszta?

*Klein:* As I said, I did not see Yugoslavian ambassador Mrazovich much from February of 1948 till the fall. Once we were at Paks at the end of September, 1948. Györgyi Tarisznyás told me that Ambassador Mrazovich and a couple

* László Rajk, central figure of the infamous show trial of 1948 orchestrated by the Communist government to convince the people that they were surrounded by traitors to their cause even from within the highest Party echelons. (At the time of his arrest, Rajk was Minister of Foreign Affars.)

of his associates would like to hunt on my estate and that I should give my consent. I said I would gladly oblige. Then Mrazovich asked that since he and his friends would be coming down to hunt by car, would I go by carriage to Route 6, the main road between Budapest and Szekszárd, because that's where the dirt road and the highway meet, that's Route 6, at the 116 kilometer mark, where there's a MÁVAÚT bus station as well. I should wait for him there and take him because you can't pass over the dirt road by car, but he asked that I drive the horses because he wants to hunt incognito. I promised. Györgyi Tarisznyás was already there, and she said Mrazovich had invited her along. After about thirty minutes Ambassador Mrazovich arrived. He got out of his car, he and a man in a green loden coat and dark glasses, whom I didn't know. After a short greeting they got in the carriage, which I drove all the way to the village limits of Biritó-puszta. We stopped at a distance from the buildings and they got off along with Györgyi Tarisznyás, and took the food and the two hunting rifles that Györgyi Tarisznyás brought along. The three of them went to the hunting field and asked me to wait for them. They came back in approximately two and a half hours and then I took them out to the main road again on the carriage. Two of them got in the car waiting for them on the main road, and then I took Györgyi Tarisznyás back to Paks by carriage.

*Presiding Judge:* What role did László Rajk play at that so-called hunt?*

*Klein:* I'm sorry but I don't know László Rajk. I didn't know him. I never saw him. Now that we had the official confrontation, that's when I recognized in him the man who was there with Mrazovich in the green loden coat and glasses.

*Presiding Judge:* Do you still recognize him as that man?

*Klein:* (after studying László Rajk at length): Yes!

*(László Rajk and his cronies before the People's Tribunal. In: Szikra, 1949)*

So then, the Hunors are presently living in the chicken coop. His parents and younger brother, Gábor, who was born in 1953, live further up, in the small old house. Hunor, when he got married in 1966, fixed up the chicken coop. It took three months, he took out a seven thousand forint bank loan, he had three thousand forints of his own, the rest were lent to him by the two sets of parents and their friends. It came to fifteen thousand forints. They now had a room that measured 4 x 4 meters, and by annexation, a 2 x 3 m. kitchen and pantry. Hunor earns two thousand forints a month on the average. His wife, a welder at the Orion plant, works for seven forints an hour, which makes for an average monthly income of one thousand three hundred forints. Now she is at home and receives six hundred forints maternity aid. Their son was born in 1967. They are paying back their loans in seven hundred forint monthly installments, but once they've paid back the price of the renovation, they will continue to shoulder this burden because they've picked out a set of furniture that costs seven thousand forints. They have only an iron bed now, on loan, and the bed for the little boy. They built themselves a tile stove and bought a cooking stove that works with a gas cylinder. There is no running water. They fetch water from the public well on the street. They have a radio and a television they got as a present. The television doesn't work, but they hope it can be fixed. The bedding, too, is just so-so, and their clothes have holes in them. That's the sum of their possessions.

Since they live in the same household with the parents and pay two-fifths of the food, the expense of eating at home has gone down to a thousand forints a month. When he goes to work, Hunor takes only fifteen forints with him per day. They have practically no rent to pay. Heating costs a hundred forints a month, gas twenty-five to thirty forints. They calculate another two hundred forints for miscellaneous expenses. In this way, they can just scrape by. The extra expense that goes towards their child, two hundred and fifty to three hundred forints per month, is basically a deficit covered by support from the parents, plus sporadic overtime. They do not consider themselves poor. By nature, Hunor firmly believes in himself. He calculates that it will take them three or four years to get over their initial difficulties. Afterwards it will be easier to keep their lifestyle on an even keel, maybe even improve it. But they are not planning any more children.

*(Sándor László-Bencsik: History from a Lower Perspective, 1973)*

# new saying

People contend that there are no new sayings these days. Still, there's been at least one exception to this rule.

In the village of B., in Heves County, they found a man (Károly Rakasza, ditch digger) who on August 7, 1640, forgot to die. He was absent minded in other ways, to be sure. For instance, he never knew who was king, and from 1655 onwards he's been living under the misconception that Emperor Leopold I is still the ruling monarch.

This probably explains why he forgot about his chronically knotted bowels. He kept digging and digging, oblivious to the excruciating pain inside him, until eventually he even forgot the name of his illness, and then the illness itself went clear out of his head. For the past four hundred years he's been as hail and hearty as you or me.

He's lost count of the number of his great, great-great, and great-great-great grandchildren, but he continues to dig up the earth, as a result of which the county is cross-crossed with a network of ditches that makes travel nearly impossible.

It was this circumstance that drew attention to the absent-minded living dead, and in B. (where his birth was entered in the records), the town council convened and brought a ruling to the effect that the digging must stop, and that the absent-minded old geezer must be reminded that – even if belatedly – it was time for him to die.

Their efforts, however, were in vain, because when the secretary of the council visited the spot where he was last seen, the ever-lively Rakasza was already digging a new ditch at an appreciable distance from him and thus could not hear him shouting. (It should be added, by way of an aside, that Rakasza was also hard of hearing, which is only natural at his age.) The council secretary has been going out to the fields ever since, and Rakasza has been digging his network of ditches ever since; the council secretary always takes off after him, but Rakasza continues digging; the council secretary continues to shout, but Rakasza still does not hear him, and this is how the new saying, "He bellows like the council secretary," was born.

# folklore

## 1. BANTER

A black limousine approaches from the direction of county headquarters. It comes to a halt. A man in black gets out and walks over to the pea fields.

"Well, well, how are we doing?" he asks the peasants by way of a joke.

"We're very well, thank you," the peasants say by way of a joke.

*(Folklore from Sárvár, Vas County, 1957)*

## 2. UNIMPEDED PRODUCTION STANDARDS

"Hello? Machine shop?"
"Skultéti here."
"How much, Skultéti?"
"Thirty-three, Comrade."
"What's thirty-three, Skultéti?"
"What's thirty-three, Comrade?"
"Yes, what's thirty-three, Skultéti."
"Why? Wasn't thirty-three the right answer, Comrade?"
"The right answer to what, Skultéti?"
"To your question, Comrade."
"Never mind, Skultéti, just resume where you left off."

*(Heavy industry folklore, 1978)*

# new lords

I'm at the hotel looking for a room. I'm standing in line in front of the hotel clerk's booth. A man wearing a suit leans in through the clerk's window in front of me. I hear only the tail end of what he's saying, no more than half a sentence, if that.

"... Just that I wouldn't like you getting into a scrape because Comrade Szalai, for instance, might have no recourse but to pick up the phone, for instance, and call the Ministry of Light Industry, because the Hotel Bakony, for instance, won't give him the best room, Comrade, if you know what I mean, for instance."

"Yes, of course," the hotel clerk nods as he proceeds to erase a name from the guest register.

*1955*

# what gives?

The J.s, a respectable family, have asked that their name be withheld. In exchange they promised to tell us their story, holding nothing back, hoping for advice from our readers.

They inherited a plot of land in the former 127th Street (now Rivalda Street), and with years of hard labor, blood, sweat and tears, built a four room family home, where they moved in last year, on the Day of Our Lady of Hungary (not that this bears with significance).

They'd come from a basement apartment. It was slightly damp, but it never bothered them, while Rivalda Street is located in a green residential area and their house faces south and is flooded with light. But they'd hardly unpacked when they began to itch.

In the first blush of happiness, they ignored the itch. At last they had everything – a house, a hot water heater, carpet beater, a TV, wall-to-wall carpeting, and many other things besides, which we will not enhance upon for lack of space. But in that case, what was going on? Nervous exhaustion, they reasoned. Considering the fact that they'd built their house with the sweat of their brow, it sounded plausible.

J., who is an engineer, worked day and night, accepted any overtime that came his way, and now lives on coffein. Mrs. J., who was in charge of the paper work and the construction workers, the loans and extra portions of wooden planks, gradually lost her grip on herself. She now swipes at the wall even when there are no flies around.

They married their daughter, in love with someone else, to a country veterinarian because their new relatives helped them out with a handsome sum of money. Their only son dreamed of becoming a doctor. But the question was: framing the roof or medical diploma?

Poor boy has been of two minds ever since. He squints perpetually, whereas he does not eat meat, and when it comes to dairy products, only processed cheese and milk. Still, he was the first whose itching became unbearable. He went to the dermatological clinic for two months, but the treatment didn't help.

It didn't help the others either. Their itching is not the type that appears in certain spots; it affects the entire surface of the body. Neither scratching nor applying a compress will alleviate it, not even sprinkling with soothing talcum powder. In the morning it is more or less bearable, but by evening, and especially by night, it is excruciating.

What gives? The life of the J.s is living hell. They go about their business in a daze. They hurry off, they hurry back. They eat standing up. They can't sit down because everything that didn't itch in their basement home, from the top of their heads, the tip of their noses, the soft inner side of their knees, you name it, is itching them now. What's worse, besides the itchy spots – their ears, for instance – the fingers they use to scratch their ears with also itch. Honest. So what gives?

They have requested that I make their counter-measures public.

They have tried all the creams and ointments that might conceivably do the trick. They use an ultraviolet light. They have fumigated their home. They have boiled every piece of clothing they own.

They have hired Dr. E.K. (who has also requested that his name be withheld) who, after going over the place with his geodesic rod, ascertained that there are no harmful magnetic fields either in or around the house.

They have recently been told that the water of the River Jordan is good for itching. They ask anyone who can get hold of Jordan water to contact them.

They also ask anyone who cannot get hold of Jordan water but has been cured of a similar ailment to contact them.

Also, anyone who has suffered from a similar ailment and has not been cured.

In fact, they request that everyone contact them and tell them what they think, because they can't go on living like this any more.

*1967*

# triplets in óbuda

## NEWSPAPERS

The eyes of the world are focused on the obstetrics ward of the Óbuda Hospital where, without any previous training, a cleaning woman from a factory brought triplets into the world. What's more, the triplets are joined at the shoulder. This beat the world record set in the 19th century, when a woman gave birth to a pair of Siamese twins, because there were just two of them, whereas to the eternal glory of all Hungarian mothers, the Óbuda triplets are three.

People have veritably laid siege to the hospital, heaping flowers, presents and good wishes on the mother who – along with her newborn babies – is in the best of health.

## TELEVISION

When it learned about the birth of the Óbuda triplets, Hungarian Television promptly cut short its scheduled programing, announced the news for the benefit of the viewers, then broadcast pictures of the Óbuda watertower as well as the sewage disposal facility, whose construction is proceeding according to plan.

The announcer cautioned all citizens against an excessive show of emotion and asked that the populace remain calm.

## STATEMENTS

I hereby wish to express my gratitude to all those who wished me luck or were kind enough to bring me presents on the occasion of the birth of my three sons, who came into the world united at the shoulder.

*Mrs. Lajos Firbejsz*

## MEDICAL OPINION

The birth of the so-called "Óbuda triplets" gave rise to much heresay. There have already been rumors of four, even five babies. In view of such nationalistic propaganda, we at the obstetrics ward feel it our civic duty to say it like it is. Undoubtely, three babies joined at the shoulder have recently come into the world, but this is not such a big deal. It could just as easily have happened in the Soviet Union or some other socialist country. They should be thought of like someone holding three knaves in his hand at cards, except the knaves are joined. We further wish to state that here, at the obstetrics ward, we did not encourage the mother to perform such an extravagant feat, and in the future will continue to deliver completely normal, single babies only.

## GOVERNMENT BULLETIN

Inside sources have borne out that the news about the Óbuda triplets have been maliciously exaggerated. The government has set up a special committee which has discovered that the Óbuda triplets consist of just one normal male child joined at the shoulder by half of another normal male child. Since there is nothing extraordinary in this, the government plans to implement no changes in its present policies. It will continue construction of the Budapest-Vienna speedway and will go on expressing its solidarity with our allies.

## INVITATION

The National Women's Association invited Mrs. Lajos Firbejsz for a friendly chat, hoping to clarify how many baby boys she actually delivered in Óbuda.

The pleasant afternoon tea stretched into the evening hours because, with understandable motherly pride, Mrs. Firbejsz would not admit, except after much persuasion, that she'd been suffering from double vision all her life. But after a time, no one laughed as hard as she when she learned that not only did she see her children double, but even the Gellért Hill; what's more, she had been laboring under the impression that there were two Women's Associations in Hungary, not to mention two political parties.

## LETTER TO THE EDITOR

I am a mother of one and a half children. Why do I have to buy two tram tickets, then, and why do I have to buy two sets of high school textbooks, when I don't have two, just one and a half sons? Also, why don't they make half cherry kisses for my half son, who loves them to distraction?

## RULING

We are sorry to inform you that your college application has been rejected because your previous studies and college entrance examination scores – in short, your exceptional scholastic abilities – may make the average students feel inferior, seeing how they've got just one brain a piece.

## POLICE ANNOUNCEMENT

A twenty year old man who left his Óbuda apartment in a highly dejected state of mind hasn't been seen since. Personal description: one blue eye, one set of sixteen teeth, a regular, semi-circular face. Special distinguishing marks: his other half is missing.

## CLASSIFIED ADVERTISEMENT

Having lost two brothers, a deeply disillusioned young man of unexceptional appearance and unexceptional mental abilities seeks the acquaintance of a young lady who will recprocate his unexceptional feelings with unexceptional feeling of her own. Respond to: "Inconspicuous."

*1969*

# a quick lesson in foreign affairs

I'd been to every fuel depot in the neighborhood, I even went to the timber-slide, but in vain. It is so difficult to obtain anything these days. Then somebody called my attention to a basement on the outskirts whose manager – a resourceful guy quick on the up and up – was said to be able to get you anything, provided you took him a bottle of rum. As luck would have it, I didn't even have to buy any. We had rum at home, real Cuban rum.

I found the basement. There were eight steps leading down to it. I hadn't gone half way with the rum in my brief-case, when a man called from below:

"Don't bother. We're fresh out of German Democratic fuel-cakes!"

I finished my descent, greeted the man, and put the rum out on the sheet-iron table covered in coal dust.

"I don't want fuel-cakes," I said.

"What do you want, then?" the man inquired with a side-ways glance at the rum.

"I'd like to get my hands on some fission material," I said.

Wherever I'd been till then, I was told in no uncertain terms that they didn't have any. But this time, the man stepped closer to the rum and examined the label, allowing his eyes to rest on the sugar-cane printed on it. Then he said:

"I might be able to scrape a bit of pitchblende ore together for you."

I laughed.

"You've got to be kidding! You don't really expect me to start hutching at home, in my own kitchen?"

I grabbed the rum and put it back in my briefcase. That did the trick.

"What's your hurry?" the man said. "Just tell me exactly what it is you're looking for. Who knows. Maybe I can help you after all."

"As if he didn't know," I thought, but I explained to him anyway – patiently, I might add – that I needed the usual radioactive element, namely, pure uranium isotope 233.

"Of course, if you don't have any," I added, "a bit of plutonium 239 might do the trick."

I took the rum out of my briefcase again and placed it on the sheet-iron table covered in coal dust. I said nothing. Neither did he. But he took the bottle of rum with him to the back and placed it inside a rickety file cabinet. What's the use of all the talk? This mute game was worth a thousand words. We both understood that the deal had been struck. The coalmerchant was being captious just for the sake of appearances.

"Have you got a carrier rocket," he asked.

"I do."

I didn't furnish the details. I knew that if I were to let on and tell him what trouble I had gone to before I found a small co-op in nearby Csillaghegy where they pieced together a medium-range rocket for me, I'd drive up the price of the fission material, and the fact that I had to part with an English-made mechanical pianino and six bolts of rough linen, plus the usual bottle of rum to get it, would not have helped in the least.

I had calculated correctly. The coal-merchant quoted me a surprisingly low price, and I proceeded to count the money out on the sheet-iron table.

"Have you got a container with you," he asked.

"I don't have one on me, no," I said.

"In that case, I need a two forint bottle deposit."

I gave him the two forints.

"Cork?" he asked.

"No cork."

He sighed. Then he tore off a bit of newspaper, rolled it up, and used it to block the neck of an unwashed mineral-water bottle which he'd taken from the rickety cabinet where he'd hidden the rum.

"Wrapped?" he asked.

"Don't bother," I said.

"Come back soon," he said, then cordially accompanied me up the steps. When we reached street level, he added:

"I hope it is for peaceful purposes."

"What else?" I said.

"I only asked because you seem like such a joker," he said, then wagged his finger at me.

*1967*

# my good old

In the state of Pennsylvania in the United States of America, there is a small town called Stockpool, and in this small town, there is a sheriff who is called Elemér Balla. He's been elected to this office five times already, which is not surprising in view of the fact that the majority of the population are Hungarian. There is also a small native English-speaking American minority, to be sure, but with rare exceptions, they also cast their ballots for Balla.

The native Americans live partly dispersed in small pockets and partly at the lower end of Fő utca (Main Street). However, this does not mean that they are cut off from the Hungarians in any way. Many of them, especially the young, are eager to learn Hungarian; what's more, every American family considers it a stroke of great good luck if they can give their daughter's hand in marriage to a Hungarian. Sheriff Balla's son, for instance, a civil engineer, hooked up with Bessie Smith, who is of real American stock, and the match was clearly made in heaven.

Weddings are the same everywhere, by which I mean that they're a source of interminable talk, whereas nothing extraordinary happens, ever. The Balla wedding was no exception. The guests were seated around three long tables set up on the manicured lawn of the Smith residence, partly Hungarians, partly Americans, three or four hundred in all, though closer to four, and they ate and drank to their hearts' delight as they engaged in lively conversation. Later, when the mood was at its height, Sheriff Balla stood up and with glass in hand, proposed a toast to the newlyweds.

Though Balla was a little worse for drink, he wished the young couple good luck, much happiness, and the patter of lots of little feet with due calm and ceremony. But then his thoughts began to wander, and he told the wedding guests that his father, who'd come from over the seas as an emigrant, had told him a story once about the Old World. In the village where his grandfather lived – the sheriff had forgotten the name of the place long ago – his grandfather held a grape harvest in his vineyard. Nobody knows what it's like in the old country, but it seems that during harvest time, the people visit one another, and on that particular occasion, too, a couple of carriages made their bumpy way up the hill to his grandfather's vineyard.

Even Sheriff Balla's father could not remember any more whether it was his grandfather's younger brother or nephew who'd come to visit; be that as it may, whoever it was had come from a great distance, or else had been away a long time and hadn't send news of himself. In short, he now came up to the top of the vineyard on a sort of cart or buggy, and then his grandfather stepped over to him, placed his two hands on his visitor's shoulder and said, *"Édes öregem, édes öregem,"* whereupon his younger brother or nephew took his grandfather's arms with both hands and began gently rocking him back and forth while he also said, *"Édes öregem, édes öregem"*. Whether his grandfather had said anything else his father couldn't remember because his memory wasn't what it used to be, but it must have been something very touching, and this made the sheriff, tough as he was, feel sentimental as well, a man who for years had commerce only with bank robbers, burglars, and murderers. But then he got a grip on himself and said that the present company mustn't be surprised, because things are different in the old country, and it's not easy to understand. For one thing, there are no Americans over there, and for another, the people don't speak anything except Hungarian. For instance, while they were holding and gently rocking each other back and forth, his grandfather repeated yet again, in Hungarian, *"Édes öregem, édes öregem."*

The wedding guests fell silent, as all eyes were rivetted on Sheriff Balla in wonder and amazement, whereas all he said was *édes öregem, édes öregem,* adding in English – unnecessarily, I might add, because all the wedding guests knew Hungarian perfectly well – *my good old fellow, my good old fellow.*

This wedding and this toast were talked about for many years to come, even if what had actually been said no one could quite remember, seeing how the simple story about the old country emerged from Sheriff Balla's memories in a rather hazy garb. Still, the Hungarians passed it on, and the Americans passed it on, too, which made a vague story vaguer still; but there must have been something to it, because those who passed it on, as well as those who heard it, remembered it for the rest of their lives, and if they encountered anyone who hadn't heard it, they were eager to tell it. And yet, oh, Lord, what was the gist of it? *Édes öregem, édes öregem,* which in English is *my good old fellow, my good old fellow,* not to mention the fact that the meaning of these words is exactly the same in both languages. So why pass it on? Who knows.

# snowy landscape, two onion domes

Actually, all of Davidovka should have been in attendance, meaning not only our battalion, but the locals as well. But this time, things were different. Only a handful of pusillanimous toadies from the battalion were there, plus the indisposed, the office personnel and the supplies people – those who had a vested interest; forty or fifty in all. The Russians were even fewer. The locals whom the duty sergeant managed to chase out of their houses stood around for a time, but as soon as they saw their chance, absconded. Still, no one was as conspicuous by his absence as battalion commander Major Holló, who was invariably present at executions, and was a great stickler for formalities. This time, though, he displayed himself in front of headquarters for a moment, looked around the church square, commented that it was cold, went back inside, and was not seen again. As a result, except for the doctor and the duty sergeant, official representation consisted only of a German truck driver and a junior officer with a Leica swung around his neck. They'd brought the prisoner to Davidovka, because the German military tribunal had said that the sentence should be carried out there. And of course, the beater Ecetes was there, too, because he had agreed to hang the prisoner for three bottles of rum. Ecetes was well into his first bottle and was thus none too stable on his legs.

The prisoner, a woman, was standing under the tree, motionless, as if her feet were frozen to the icy ground. Her eyes were dry. In our experience, the elderly die with the greatest ease. They panic and are alarmed, as if they couldn't quite make out what is happening to them, but they don't beg, they don't cry, they don't scream. This woman was still quite young, quite attractive, and quite well dressed, yet not a word of complaint passed her lips. She just stood there, her gaze intently pinned on a little girl who'd climbed under the truck and was now peeking out from under it. She must have been four or five. She was dirty and scrawny, but was also well dressed in a small fur vest, quilted pants, thick cotton socks, and rubber boots. When they hooked the noose around the young woman's neck, she gave a brief, gleeful laugh from under the truck, as if someone had tickled her.

Three minutes later the army doctor declared the woman dead. A cold wind that had sprung up began to sway the young woman's body back and forth. The little girl climbed out from under the truck. She watched the swaying motion for a while and then, as if she'd decided that she'd had enough of the joke, called up at the tree, "Mother!"

There wasn't a single Russian in front of the church by then, while from among us there were only the beater Márton Ecetes, the duty sergeant Elek Bíró, the battalion physician Dr. Tibor Friedrich, and a corporal called István Koszta, otherwise the barman of the Golden Bull Hotel, who'd repeatedly asked to be assigned to a hospital someplace in the rear of the front because of his carbuncles. Now, too, he positioned himself so the doctor would notice the red boils on his neck. But Doctor Friedrich turned away and looked into the lens of the Leica. The German junior officer waved to the little girl to get out of the picture, but she would not budge from where she stood. She just stared bright and round eyed into the Leica because, possibly, she had never seen a camera before.

# paris, à bientôt!

My suitcase was heavy, but I dragged it down to Rue des Écoles, where I hailed a cab.

"The Gare de l'Est," I told the driver.

I had plenty of time, and I didn't want to wait at the station, so I added, "I'm going home. But first, will you have a farewell drink with me?"

"I have only half a stomach," he said.

"A glass of white wine won't hurt you," I reassured him.

"I know a place," he said.

We clinked glasses and drank the wine, then he ordered another round. As we waited, he asked, "What do you call home?"

"Budapest."

"Where is that?"

"Hungary."

"With or against the Germans?"

"With," I said.

"Not good," he said.

"Not good," I seconded.

The proprietor brought the wine.

"They should send the government ministers to the front," the driver said after some reflection.

"Indeed," I said. "That would get them thinking."

We paid and left. He insisted on taking my suitcase up the steps of the Gare de l'Est, then offered his hand.

"I was disqualified because of my stomach," he said.

"You were lucky," I said.

"Don't you have any illness?" he said.

"No," I said.

"Never mind," he said by way of comfort. "Two months, and we'll have the Germans running for their lives."

"I hope so," I said.

"Who knows. Maybe we'll meet again," he added.

"If only we could," I said.

"And we'll have another glass of wine," he said.

"You bet," I said.

"À bientôt," he went on.

"À bientôt," I said.

*1963*

# banner

The People's Republic of Hungary
The People's Republic of Hunga
The People's Republic of Hu
The People's Republic of
The People's Republic
The People's Repub
The People's Re
The People's
The People'
The Peo
The P
The
The
The
The
The
The
The
The
The
The
The
The
The

*1975*

# perpetuum mobile

Auspitz told us he was a baker's assistant on Veress Pálné Street back home. He told us that he'd eat a two-pound loaf of bread every morning, just for the heck of it, and he used to weigh two-hundred pounds.

"How much do you think I weigh now?" he asked.

We couldn't say. As things stood, he didn't even use the toilet any more, which was a bad sign, and he only drank water, which was even worse. He kept drinking water. He wasn't even thirsty, but he kept downing it like a drain.

His clothes were covered with lice eggs – another bad sign. The only way to curb lice is to keep killing them, otherwise they multiply and fill the folds of your garments with their nit, especially around the warm, moist parts of the body. Auspitz's armpits had turned gray from the lice eggs, but we didn't say anything. At such a juncture, words are of no avail.

One night he was moving about so restlessly, I woke up.

"What are you doing, Auspitz?"

"I'm eating."

"What are you eating, Auspitz?"

"I'm eating lice eggs, old man. And lice."

I lit a match, but blew it out. The front had come so close we weren't even allowed to smoke at night. But I caught a glimpse of his face. It was serene, sedate. I said to him:

"Don't talk nonsense, Auspitz."

"You want me to wait until they suck my life's blood away?" he said.

He explained that we had two weeks to hold out, if that, and if he eats the lice, he'll survive the two weeks with ease, because this way nothing will go to waste. Every drop of blood that the lice suck from him is returned to his body, and in this way, he will grow neither weaker, nor stronger.

"If that's the case," I said, "you have invented the perpetuum mobile."

He had no idea what that was. I explained that it's something that doesn't need energy. He still didn't catch on. As he ate the nit, I explained the perpetuum mobile to him. After a while, we fell asleep. In the morning I tried to shake him awake, but he was gone.

*1967*

# let's learn foreign languages

I don't speak German. Somewhere between Budgonnii and Alexaieva we had to haul heavy artillery up a hill, because they were fast sinking into the mud. When it was my turn again, for the third time, and the son of a bitch field gun started rolling back down just as I thought I'd made it to the top, I pretended I had to answer the call of nature, and absconded.

I knew my way back to camp. I cut across a huge sunflower field and soon reached the stubble. The rich black soil clung to my boots the way a lead weight clings to a deep-sea diver when he descends to the bottom. I must have been trodding along for twenty minutes when I ran into a Hungarian sergeant and a German officer whose rank I couldn't make out since I had no familiarity with German military insignia. Running into anyone, let alone these two, on that flat terrain, was in itself an incredible stroke of bad luck.

The sergeant, who was standing, was smoking a cigarette. The German officer was sitting on a small camp chair, his legs spread wide, and he was squeezing some sort of cheese spread atop a slice of bread from something that looked like a tube of tooth paste. When he saw me, he motioned me to stop.

*"Was sucht er hier?"* he asked.

"What are you doing here?" the sergeant translated.

I said I got cut off from my outfit.

*"Er hat seine Einheit verloren,"* the sergeant said. He lost his unit.

*"Warum ohne Waffe?"*

"Where is your gun?" the sergeant asked.

I said I was in a forced labor battalion.

*"Jude,"* the sergeant said.

Even I understood that. I explained that I was not Jewish, and that I had been assigned to a special forced labor unit for being the local distributor of a leftist paper in the city of Győr.

*"Was?"* the German asked.

*"Jude,"* the sergeant said.

The German got up, brushing the bread crumbs off his jacket.

*"Ich werde ihn erschiessen,"* he said.

"The *Feldwebel* will now shoot you," the sergeant translated.

By now I was drenched in sweat, and I was beginning to feel sick to my stomach. The German screwed back the cap on the tube of cheese spread and took out his gun. Perhaps if I spoke German, I could have explained to him that since I'm not wearing a yellow armband, I can't be a Jew, and then things would have taken a different turn.

*"Er soll zehn Schritte weiter gehen."*

"Move on ten paces," the sergeant ordered.

I did as I was told and found myself ankle deep in mud.

*"Gut."*

"Good."

I stopped. The *Feldwebel* aimed his gun at me. I can still remember how all of a sudden my head felt unbearably heavy and I thought my insides would burst. The *Feldwebel* lowered his gun.

*"Was ist sein letzter Wunsch?"* he asked.

"A last wish?" the sergeat translated.

I said I needed to move my bowels.

*"Er will scheissen,"* the sergeant translated.

*"Gut."*

"All right."

While I was relieving myself, the *Feldwebel* leaned on his gun. As soon as I straightened up, he raised it.

*"Fertig?"* he asked.

"Finished?"

"Finished," I said.

*"Fertig,"* the lance sergeant translated.

The *Feldwebel*'s gun must have had a way of kicking upwards, because he aimed at my navel. I stood motionless for a minute or so. Then, as he continued pointing his gun, he said,

*"Er soll hüpfen."*

"Start hopping," the sergeant translated.

The hopping was followed by a crawl. Then I was told to do fifteen pushups. After that, the *Feldwebel* ordered me to do an about-face.

I did as I was told.

*"Stechschritt!"*

"Goose-step!" the sergeant said.

*"Marsch!"* the *Feldwebel* screamed.

"Forward march!" the lance sergeant translated.

I tried to march, but it was no use. I had trouble enough walking, let alone doing the goose-step, as balls of mud were flying over my head. My advance was maddeningly slow, and all the while I could feel the *Feldwebel*'s gun aimed at the small of my back. I could point to the spot to this very day. If it hadn't been for the mud, my ordeal wouldn't have lasted more than five minutes. But under the circumstances, it took at least half an hour before I dared to drop on my stomach and look back.

I don't speak any Italian either. In fact, I have no ear for languages. When I visited Rimini last summer on a ten-day tour organized by the State Travel Agency, I spotted the *Feldwebel* one evening in front of a luxury hotel called the Regina Palace. However, luck was not with me. Had I reached the spot just half a minute earlier, I'd have beaten him within an inch of his life. But as things stood, he didn't even know I was there, and when he and his group boarded a red bus with a glass roof I, lacking command of foreign languages, was reduced to screaming in Hungarian, "Stop! Get that fascist son of a bitch off that bus!"

The doorman, a tall, robust Sudanese, shook his finger at me and motioned to me to scram, and me, I couldn't even explain to him what had just happened, even though he probably spoke some French and English as well as Italian while I, alas, speak nothing but my native Hungarian.

*1966*

# appetite

Far, far away, beyond the double barbed wire fence, a sled came into view. Like in a fairy tale, it was drawn by two small hairy horses, and it was driven by a small man in a big hairy hat. It was laden with round-backed loaves of black bread that made our mouths water, even from a distance.

It came three times a week, but every time it came, all eight thousand of us watched it approach. Sometimes it brought skinned horses heads grinning, yellow toothed, at us from a distance. Sometimes it brought salted fish or millet or tinned food. It felt good to watch it, even if watching it did us no good, because as soon as it reached the camp gate, the sled turned in the direction of the warehouses, where a hefty portion of the food was invariably stolen.

That day, though, things took a different turn. A miracle, but the gate opened up, and the small man in the hairy hat made for the *lagerstrasse,* the main road of the camp. Instantly, the camp came alive with a great rumble, as if the earth had split in two.

The camp had four streets. The barracks squatted in eight rows sunk deep in the snow. The doors opened, and the roads filled up with people, an army of black ants teaming towards the open gate.

It didn't take long.

Billowing and surging on top like a sea of worms, the army of black ants swarmed around the sled. For a minute or two they crawled, trampling each other under foot, then they headed back over the main road in droves, dispersed along the side streets, and disappeared inside the barracks. Only the sled remained.

The sled remained, but the bread was gone, and so were the two little hairy horses, and the little driver in the hairy hat. Only the empty sled, the whip handle, and the parts of the horse gear not made of leather, this is all that remained – a couple of chains and buckles and rings. Oh, and a cluster of keys.

# in memoriam dr. h. g. k.

*"Hölderlin ist ihnen unbekannt?"** Dr. H.G.K. asked as he dug the pit for the horse's carcass.

"Who is that?" the German guard growled.

"The author of *Hyperion,"* said Dr. H.G.K., who had a positive passion for explanations. "The greatest figure of German Romanticism. How about Heine?" he tried again.

"Who're them guys?" the guard growled, louder than before.

"Poets," Dr. H.G.K. said. "But Schiller. Surely you have heard of Schiller?"

"That goes without saying," the German guard nodded.

"And Rilke?" Dr. H.G.K. insisted.

"Him, too," the German guard said and, turning the color of paprika, shot Dr. H.G.K. in the back of the head.

* You're not familiar with Hölderlin?" [Germ.]

# home sweet home

The little girl was only four and her memories were correspondingly vague. In order to refresh them, her mother took her up to the barbed wire fence and pointed to the wagons standing at a distance.

"Can you see?" she said. "That train is going to take us home."

"Is that good?" the little girl asked.

"Yes, it's good," her mother said. "We'll see our home again."

"What's home?" the little girl asked.

"The place where we once lived," her mother said.

"So what?" the little girl asked.

"You remember your Teddy bear? And your dolls? Maybe you still have your dolls."

"Mommy," the little girl asked, "will we have guards there, too?"

"No, dear," her mother said, "no guards."

"Does that mean," the little girl asked, "that we'll be able to escape?"

# the best
# of all possible worlds

*For Tibor Déry**

"Why am I silent, you ask?"

"Yes. Why?"

"Because I can think of nothing to say," he says, blowing his nose. "It is a state of pure bliss."

"Most of us are the same way," I say. "A happy nation."

"Happy times," he says. "Because, should anyone happen to think of something sensible to say, it would only perfect the best of all possible worlds, which is nonsense, of course, seeing how perfection is not subject to degrees, in which case, should anyone think of anything sensible to say, our world could not then be the best of all possible worlds."

"In which case, what would happen?" I ask.

"In which case, I would also think of something to say," he says.

"And…?"

"Nothing," he says.

"In which case, indubitably, this is the best of all possible worlds," I say.

*1978*

* Tibor Déry (1894-1977) was among the group of writers who during the revolution of 1956 wholeheartedly supported the popular revolt. He was revered for his passionate love of truth. The price he paid was nine years' imprisonment.

# survival

As a second defendant in a major political trial, he had been sentenced for life and spent six years in solitary, even though he was innocent. His mates succumbed one by one, each hit in his weakest spot, the heart, the lungs, the psyche. His weak spot was his nerves, and so by the sixth week he suffered a crying fit. However, just as he collapsed over the tabletop, he saw an ant, and he found the sight so intriguing, he forgot his tears. For a while he watched the ant struggle with a minuscule crumb of bread, then carefully, with the tip of a finger nail, he began flicking the crumb further and further away, making the ant crawl around the table all morning.

At night, he placed the ant inside an empty medicine bottle, but the following morning, he made it climb up a matchstick. He soon realized that it would be much easier to train the small creature with a shred of meat rather than a crumb of bread, and by the end of the eighth month, he managed to get it to see-saw on top of two diagonally placed matchsticks. Though that dubious swaying back and forth could hardly be called see-sawing, not even with the best of intentions, still, his achievement made him happy.

Because of good conduct, at the end of his third year he was allowed to ask for paper, pen, and reading materials, but proud and defiant, he rejected the offer, because by then the ant could roll a poppy seed, the remnant of his Christmas roll, back and forth. But this quite remarkable feat still did not satisfy him, because it lay well within the bounds of an ordinary ant's existence. He wanted his ant to stand on two legs. It took eighteen months, but his efforts paid off.

In another eighteen months, just as he'd managed his greatest feat, and while standing on its hind legs the ant could throw the poppy seed up in the air and catch it, he was discretely told that he'd be discharged and rehabilitated.

After his first dinner at home, he turned to his sons. "Hand me a magnifying glass," he announced with an enigmatic smile. "I have a trained ant!"

"Where?" his wife asked.

They turned the medicine bottle round and round. They studied it with the magnifying glass. Nothing. But strangest of all, he couldn't see it either any more.

*1968*

# fate

Somewhere on the Great Hungarian Plain there once lived a family on a small farm. The family consisted of the father, the mother, and their two small children, all of whom loved crackling scones. If the mother had time to spare and wanted to please her family, she would bake them a big plate of crackling scones.

But one day instead of flour, she kneaded rat poison into the dough. It was none the worse for taste and the family ate their fill of the scones and so, by morning all four were dead, the father, the mother, and their two small children.

Four days later they were buried, and their relatives and neighbors gathered from far and wide for the wake, as was the custom at the time, and they tasted the local wine and ate of the leftover crackling scones, too, and soon they were all dead, down to the last man.

By the time the ambulance people showed up – the medic, the two stretcher bearers and the driver – it was too late. All they could do was walk around the dead and shake their heads. But before they left, they also ate some of the crackling scones, washing them down with the local wine.

Only the driver did not eat anything. He couldn't drink wine because he was driving, and as for the crackling scones, he didn't particularly care for them. On the other hand, he took the leftovers from the plate, wrapped them in newspaper, and placed them on the seat next to him, so they shouldn't go to waste. Someone would surely eat them.

And now there they are, on the driver's seat by his side!

*1975*

# the long march

Once upon a time, a long, long time ago, there lived an egg, and this egg took it into its head to see the world. It marched on and on until it ran into King Kalimba. The king asked the egg, "Where to, egg old buddy?"

"I'm off to see the world," the egg replied.

"Wait for me, I'm coming with you," the king said.

The egg rolled on, and King Kalimba skipped along by his side, when a one wheeled bicycle came rolling along. The bicycle asked King Kalimba, "Where to, Kalimba old buddy?"

"I'm off to see the world," King Kalimba replied.

"Wait for me, I'm coming with you," the one wheeled bicycle said.

The egg rolled on, King Kalimba skipped along by his side, and the one wheeled bicycle rolled along with them. Soon they met the Holy Trinity.

"Where to, one wheeled bicycle, old buddy," the Holy Trinity asked.

"I'm off to see the world," the one wheeled bicycle replied.

"Wait for me, I'm coming with you," the Holy Trinity said.

As they walked along, they ran into Bertolt Brecht.

"Where to, Holy Trinity, old buddy," Bertolt Brecht asked.

"I'm off to see the world," the Holy Trinity replied.

"Wait for me, I'm coming with you," Bertolt Brecht said.

So Brecht got in back of the line. They'd gone quite a ways when Takariko Kiriwi, the Japanese table tennis champion, also chanced along.

"Where to, Bertolt Brecht old buddy," Kiriwi, who was wearing a pair of thick glasses, asked.

"I'm off to see the world," Brecht replied.

"Wait for me, I'm coming with you," Kiriwi said.

Up front marched the egg, behind it King Kalimba, then the one wheeled bicycle, then Jesus, Mary, and St. Joseph, followed by Bertolt Brecht, with Takariko Kiriwi, the table tennis champion, bringing up the rear. They marched on and on, and they are still marching with never a word unless, in the course of all that marching, they've died.

*1963*

# our sons

Many years ago there lived a poor old widow, and this poor old widow had two handsome sons. One of them, the first-born, entered service on a ship that headed straight for the Pacific, but nobody knows what became of him, because there's no one left to tell us, they've all disappeared without a trace.

The younger of the two sons stayed home. But once when his poor old mother sent him for some tapeworm lozenges (to the pharmacy, the seventh house from their miserable hut), he never returned. He, too, disappeared without a trace.

This is a true story, because in folk tales the poor old widow always has three sons, and the third invariably makes good.

*1968*

# tempting providence

The proper way to drive a nail into a given object is, first and foremost, to settle on the place –a wall, a plank, etcetera. Next, take the nail between two fingers of the left hand and place it exactly where you want it to go. Be sure that it is at a 90 degree angle!

Next, strike the nail with the hammer you are holding in your right hand. *Note:* Hitting the nail once will not do. The proper way to go about it is to strike the nail repeatedly in a quick, even-tempered rhythm, neither too fast nor too slow, yet with energetic and well-aimed blows. In the meantime, do not take your eye from the head of the nail, otherwise it will wobble and come loose before you know it. But if you follow instructions, it will burrow its way into the wall straight and will remain securely in place.

You may experience some difficulty at first, but don't despair. For instance, you may miss the mark and end up with your finger absorbing the blow, or bending the nail. If this happens, just discard it and try with a new nail. With time and sufficient practice, you won't even have to keep an eye on the nail, because we all have a dormant capacity to hit the nail on the head even when we don't mean to.

Once we have reached this stage, we have reached the highest level of artistry with regard to hammering a nail into an object. It is the most that can be achieved in this regard. To go further is to temp providence because with our mortal strength, frail nervous system and limited knowledge, this is as far as we can go, and no further.

Needless to say, there are some very rare exceptions. On June 7, 1927, in San Diego, California, a citrus fruit dealer by the name of J. E. Bringham drove a hammer into his fruit crates with a nail, and not a nail with a hammer, while in Madras, India, a person who wishes to remain anonymous can drive a nail into mahogany, one of the hardest woods known to man, without a single blow of the hammer, just by looking at it.

All this is impressive, but it is not for us. We should be satisfied to drive a nail into something by holding it between two fingers of the left hand while hammering it in with the right, the way we have been taught.

*1969*

# the hallowed halls of science

A young woman collapsed in front of the so-called Red Plush Room of the Hungarian Academy of Sciences. This occurred just as the hundred and seventy learned doctors who'd been to a lecture by Nobel Prize winning biologist Gunnar Ingridsson came streaming out of the room. The young woman was writhing in spasms, foaming at the mouth, and banging her head against the floor.

The Hungarian scientists were taken by surprise and started running up and down, experimenting with various medicines. They called for an ambulance and even a fire engine, for they wanted to do all they could for the young woman, especially in the presence of such an illustrious guest from abroad. They even hanged her out the window, in case she'd swallowed a pebble. But the young woman continued thrashing about, foaming at the mouth and gritting her teeth until Gunnar Ingridsson stepped in.

"Shouldn't we give her a glass of water?"

No one had thought of it, but it did the trick, and the girl regained her consciousness, calmed down, and went back to cleaning the window as if nothing had happened.

Just then, however, some TV reporters showed up, and asked the Nobel Prize recipient to step in front of the camera with half a glass of water in his hand. They also asked the girl to throw herself about one more time, and try foaming at the mouth, which went like a breeze.

Unfortunately, the second time around they could not stop the spasms, and the foam, too, issued from the girl in profusion, even though the illustrious scientist had given her not only what was left of the water, but a glass of seltzer, too. But to no avail. What could have possibly gone wrong?

*1969*

# the old man and the great big automobile

The following story may not be true, but stories that are not true deserve our attention, too, because it's the way stories are told that's enlightening. Anyone telling this particular story five years ago would have told it in the following way:

An old man is walking, ragged and barefooted, along the road from Balaton. After a while he starts waving his arm, because he sees a great big automobile come along. The great big automobile stops, and the driver opens the door.

"Why are you waving, Comrade?" he asks.

"Where are you headed?" the old man inquires.

"We're heading up to Budapest, Comrade."

"Would you kindly take me with you?" the old man asks.

"There's no room in the car, Comrade," the driver says, slams the door, and steps on the gas.

Now, as the sun is shining, the blue lake is sparkling and we are exchanging many good stories with each other, this story, too, comes up again, but in a new guise:

An old man is walking, ragged and barefooted, along the road from Balaton, when a great big automobile comes along. The great big automobile stops and the driver opens the door.

"Are you headed for Budapest, old man?" he asks.

"Yes," the old man says.

"Get in, old man, we'll take you along," the driver says with a friendly smile.

The old man goes over, sticks his head in the window, and asks:

"Have you got a radio?"

Both stories are good, but neither story is true. The truth is that the old man, ragged and barefooted, is walking along the road when there comes a great big automobile, but it never occurs to him to wave, nor does it ever occur to the driver to stop.

This is the true story. On the other hand, it is not as good as the other two.

*1955*

# room, adobe wall, thatched roof

The old bag was sitting on the side of the bed. Her face was etched in deep grooves, but her teeth were pearly white, courtesy of the social services up in Eger. The whole set. Mrs. Kászony, née Hanna Kakas, smiled, then held the microphone up to her.

"Go on, dear, don't be shy. Go on with your stories. Tell them just like before, neither louder nor softer. This machine is here to record the quaint old stories you've been telling us."

"You don't have to explain," the old hag's grandson said. He was lying on the other bed in a pair of silesia pants, reading a work of Balzac from the Cheap Library series. "The old woman was on TV last spring. Live."

"In that case, go on, dear," Mrs. Kászony, née Hanna Kakas said to the old hag by way of encouragement, then called over to me, "Record!"

I started the tape, and the old hag began telling her tale without the least sign of self-consciousness. Her breath was even, her Palócz dialect barely just there. She told the story of Bálint Kiss Puki, the swarthy and fearless village blacksmith who was frightened to death by a succubus on the frozen river by the Hadik bridge.

"You mean incubus, don't you, dear" Mrs. Kászony, née Hanna Kakas asked.

"As far as I know, it's a succubus, dear heart," said the old hag.

"Then succubus it is. But what sort of creature is a succubus?"

"I've seen many kinds of succubus, dear heart. Some were as thin as the tail end of a whip trailing a whole comet behind, others were as diminutive as a mouse's tail, with lights no bigger on top than the flame of a stuck match. They're all different. For instance, we had a succubus dash across the yard yesterday that was as big as the church tower."

"Did you see it with your own eyes, mam?" Mrs. Kászony, née Hanna Kakas asked.

The question surprised the old bag so much, her social security teeth clinked together. She gaped at Mrs. Kászony, née Hanna Kakas.

"Why do you ask," she said after a while, "haven't you ever seen a succubus, dear heart?"

"As a matter of fact, I haven't," Mrs. Kászony, née Hanna Kakas said cautiously, "I always thought they were part of folklore."

"Where do you work, dear heart?" the old hag asked, even more surprised than before, if possible.

"At the University of Sciences, mam."

"Well, I'll be," said the old bag with a shake of the head. "My eldest grandson goes there too. What is our Jóska majoring in?" she asked turning to the other bed. "It keeps slipping my mind."

"Cybernetics," her grandson in the silesia pants said, without so much as looking up from *Cousine Bette*.

# the loudspeaker

In the pool's changing room the walls are packed from floor to ceiling with lockers. One key opens them all. The attendant goes around locking and unlocking them, depending on whether someone wishes to stash his clothes away, or get them out after a swim. The attendant has been going back and forth among the lockers for thirty-five years. He could find any one of them with his eyes closed.

Sometimes the pool is practically empty. At such times he sits down for a bit of rest and listens to the music coming through the loudspeaker. At other times the newcomers and the swimmers dripping with water crowd in on him. He calls this a stampede. During a stampede he has his hands full. Other than that, being a locker room attendant holds no surprises for him. It is a simple and undemanding job, but difficult all the same. It's jobs that don't necessarily call for us to be human that are difficult.

"We've had quite a stampede just now," he comments when he sees me.

"I've been keeping an eye on you, Mr. Schuller. You practically haven't kept anybody waiting."

"It comes with practice. Of course, in a stampede like this, some attendants my age tend to lose their head."

"Are you saying experience is not enough?"

"Not always. Being a cabin attendant takes a certain natural aptitude."

"You know that better than I, Mr. Schuller."

"In fact, even natural aptitude is not enough. It takes special gifts not to lose your head in a stampede."

"What sort of gifts, Mr. Schuller?"

"You've got to stay calm. You need a booming voice and a commanding, forceful presence. Of course, such things are rarely called for."

"I suppose you've had a chance to try it, Mr. Schuller."

"There was a stampede once. If it weren't for me, people would have trampled each other underfoot."

"When was that?"

"When the loudspeaker announced the declaration of war. To make matters worse, the sun was shining and the pool was crowded with people."

Today, too, the sun is shining, the pool is crowded, and the loudspeaker is on, announcing the news.

Mr. Schuller steps over to the window. He listens. I give him a quizzical look.

"It's nothing," he says with a dismissive wave, "just a place called Bengal."

*1972*

# final solution

I'm twenty-six. I'm on the spare and wiry side, but not unattractive in appearance. All the same, I've only had three men in my life. They were all called Eugene – a coincidence, probably. And now my phone won't stop ringing. An insistent and aggressive male voice keeps asking, "Is that you, Lulika, hello, Lulika, why won't you speak to me?" I'm completely at a loss. Should I answer, or hang up? What's the smart, the correct thing to do?

I'm past thirty, but only one man has ever said he loved me. I said three just now, but I was stretching the truth. There was only one, and even he wasn't called Eugene. Afterwards the phone wouldn't stop ringing, but I've already said that, but then the phone company sent a repairman, he took it apart, "There won't be any more wrong numbers," he said, and as a matter of fact, this is the first time the phone has rung in years. Oh, dear, what if they'll be wanting to speak with Lulika? Should I say, "This is she?" Or should I say it's the wrong number and they should stop molesting me, and my name is Edit Steier?

The years pass, and so does life, and I'm still a virgin. Before rain, I get headaches. Once I was positively certain that a man called Eugene had fallen in love with me, but he was so afraid of being rejected. He called me only by phone. However, it wasn't love, because as it later turned out, my telephone was playing tricks on me again. That nearly led to a nervous breakdown, but after a while I realized I could make do with a lot less, just as long as the solution was final.

That's when I swallowed the elevator key. I attached a string to it and tied the other end to my lower eye-tooth, which stands alone, there's no tooth either to the right or the left of it. Except, I forgot that thin strings don't show up on X-rays. "You silly thing," the doctor scolded me after my surgery, "why didn't you say the key was tied to your tooth? I could have pulled it out through your mouth." But then I explained to him that I didn't mean to inconvenience him and I wasn't thinking of surgery at all, but that I *was* thinking of a solution that, while it would prove final, would not prove lethal into the bargain.

*1969*

# the relativity of fear

Two flies – ordinary domestic house flies hardly different from their fellows – would run into each other every now and then and, hanging head down from the ceiling, which is the custom in these parts, would relate to each other in the minutest detail everything that had happened to them, both good and bad.

"How are you, friend?" one would ask the other.

"I couldn't be worse, thank you," the other would reply.

Attention! Flies are notorious fibbers. What they say mustn't be taken at face value. At the same time, overstatements can be revealing.

"As a matter of fact, you don't look so good."

"No wonder. Do you want to hear?"

The other did, and the first told him how just two days before, on Sunday, the worst day of his life, he was peacefully perched atop some horse droppings in the pleasant autumn sunshine in front of the rebuilt Municipal Grand Circus where – it being Sunday – car traffic was scarce.

"And you're complaining?" the other said, surprised. "I don't get to see horse droppings for weeks on end."

"You haven't heard my story yet," the first said.

Then he explained that while he was sitting there, he suddenly heard a horrible din, a spine-chilling roar, an ear-splitting howl and the stampede of running feet, and he didn't even have time to realize what was happening, when a monstrous form came crashing out of the circus, a savage beast, a nightmare, and made straight for him.

"Go on! Go on! Don't keep me in suspense," the other said, trembling in every limb.

"Okay, I won't," the first one said, "but let me do a countdown. Ten, nine, eight, seven, six, five, your, three, two, one... And may the Lord be praised, that monster charged past no more than three feet, if that, from where I was sitting on the horse dropping!"

"But what kind of monster was it," the other asked.

"A lion," the first said. "But why are you shaking like that?"

"Because I thought it was a swallow," the other said with a sigh of relief.

They laughed, took their leave of each other, and flew their separate ways.

PRAYER

*Heavenly Father! Pray for us cowardly men who are scared of every roaring, howling, growling and charging lion, whereas it's the swallow and nothing but the swallow that is of danger to us. O Merciful Lord, save our mortal souls from these swallows. Amen.*

*1972*

# the people of técső

The reporter climbed up the scaffolding, and gingerly balancing himself on a precarious plank, he took his snapshots from up there. In this way he could get Gábor Bogya in the middle of the frame, while the pit, the brigade, and the conveyor belts also showed.

The reporter was very young. He was also agile. And ambitious. The fountain pen in his hand glided over his notepad as if he were writing in air.

"Well then, let's hear," he said after he'd climbed down from the scaffolding. "It's okay to write about bad things now, as well as the good. Did the ambulance take the injured man away?"

"They just dressed his wounds," Bogya told him. "Then he came with us to the workers' hostel."

"I may not even end up writing a report about this," the journalist said with some excitement, "I may actually write a radio play. In short, how did the fight break out?"

While he was in front of the camera, Bogya took off his greasy construction worker's cap. Now he put it back on and glanced down into the pit as he spoke.

"Somebody," he said, "started not liking the common till."

"What do you menn?"

"Share and share alike. Each of us gets paid equally by common consent."

"Which is not right," the journalist commented.

"We think it is," Bogya said. "We're from Técső."

"What do you mean?" the journalist asked, trying to make sense of what he'd heard. "Do you all work equally hard?"

"More or less."

"Isn't there anyone not as strong as the rest? Or not as good?"

"It happens."

"For instance?"

Bogya glanced down into the pit, where the men were trenching the lowest level just then.

"It's hard to say," Bogya mused.

"Is it also hard to say who is the strongest?" the journalist urged. "Because he's drawing the short end of the stick, it seems to me."

Bogya looked at the journalist. He had a rugged physique, all tendon and muscle, like the trunk of a palm. His forehead could have stopped a locomotive. Then he said:

"It's not the strength that counts."

"What then?"

"The determination. If somebody tries hard, we give him lighter work to do. If he doesn't, he's free to go."

"Has that ever happened?"

"Once."

"From Técső?"

"From Técső."

"Who was he?"

"I can't remember."

"You can't remember much, can you," the journalist said with irritation. "But you do remember the fight?"

A wrinkle ran up Bogya's forehead.

"Yeh, I remember the fight."

"Well, who started it?" the journalist asked. "Or have you forgotten that, too?"

Bogya looked down into the pit again.

"Why would you want to put that in?"

"You should appreciate the fact that we can publish things like this in the papers now."

"I do," Bogya said. "Except, we're all from Técső here. Honest, hard-working men who work the soil back home. We live at the same workers' hostel. We eat together, and when it comes to being paid, we share and share alike."

The journalist cut him short. His fountain pen was moving faster and faster, as if he were doing shorthand in the air.

"I heard that before," he said. "But wasn't it you men who got into that fight in the pub?"

"That's right." Bogya conceded.

"And wasn't it you men who called the ambulance?"

"That's right," Bogya said.

"And wasn't it you men who reported it to the police?"

"That's right," Bogya nodded.

"And what became of the guy?"

"He joined another brigade."

"Then why can't you tell me his name?"

"Because he's back," Bogya said.

"He's back?" the journalist asked with surprise. "Point him out."

"You wouldn't be able to spot him from up here," Bogya said as he glanced down into the pit one last time, "because his bandages are off."

*1962*

# budapest

A bus crashed into a tree on Calvin Square, and soon after, every tram in the city came to a halt. Everything stopped, even the toy train in the window of the toy shop. Silence everywhere. A little later there was a rasping sound, but it was just a page from a newspaper being swept along by a gust of wind. Then it was flung against a wall, and the silence grew profounder still.

Eight minutes after the atomic bomb exploded the electricity failed and immediately afterwards the last gramophone recording wound down over the radio. An hour later the water taps gave off a slurping sound, and then there was no more water. The boughs, too, became as dry as a hot tin roof. The semaphore gave the go-ahead, but the last express from Vienna never made it to the station. By morning, the water in the boiler of its locomotive was cold.

Within a month, the parks were overgrown with weed, and the sand boxes on the children's playgrounds sprouted oats. The delicious drinks, too, evaporated on the innkeepers' shelves. All the foodstuffs, all the leather goods and library books were chewed up by the mice. Mice are extremely prolific; they litter up to five times a year. In a short while they overran the streets, covering the pavement like some velvety, mud colored, billowing stonework.

They took possession of the flats, the beds in the flats, the rows of seats in the theatres. They even flooded the Opera House, where *La Traviata* had been the last performance.

When they gnawed through the last string of the last violin, that twang sounded the swan song of Budapest.

But by the following day, across the street from the Opera, attached to the stone ruins of a building, a sign appeared:

"Dr. Mrs. Varsányi, mouse exterminator. You bring the bacon, I catch the mice."

*1967*

# one minute biography

When I was born, I was such a beautiful baby the doctor swept me up in his arms and going from room to room, showed me off to the entire hospital. I even smiled, they say, which made the mothers of the other babies sigh with envy.

This happened in 1912, shortly before the outbreak of the First World War, and it was my only uncontested success, I think. From then on my life has been one of continual decline. Not only did I lose much of my extreme good looks, but some of my hair and a few of my teeth as well. What's more, I haven't been able to live up to what the world has expected of me.

I could not carry my plans into effect, nor make full use of my gifts. Though I had always wanted to be a writer, my father, who was a pharmacist, insisted I follow in his footsteps. But, even that did not satisfy him. He took it into his head that I should have a better life than his own. So after I became a pharmacist, he sent me back to college to make a chemical engineer of me. This meant another four and a half years of delay before I could indulge my passion for writing.

I had hardly put pen to paper when the war broke out. Hungary declared war on the Soviet Union, and I was taken to the front. Here, our army was made short shrift of and I found myself a prisoner of the Russians, a POW. This took another four and a half years out of my life. And when I returned home I was faced with yet further trials which did nothing to ease my way towards a career in writing.

From this it will be seen that what I was able to create under the circumstances, a couple of novels of various lengths, five or six volumes of short stories and two plays, I created more or less in secret, and I did so in the precious few hours I was able to wrench from the inexorable march of history. Perhaps this is why I have always striven for economy and precision, looking for the essence, often in haste. Startled by every ringing of the door bell, I had no reason, ever, to expect anything good either from the mailman or from any other arrival.

This also explains why, though as a new-born babe I may have attained to a perfection of sorts, from that time on I began to lose my luster, to slip and falter, and despite the circumstance that I became better at my trade and gained more and more self-knowledge, I have always been painfully aware of the impossibility of living up to my full potential.

*1968*

Printed and bound in Hungary